"Let's Switch Bodies!"

"My life—it's all falling apart today," I told Lucy. "Everything. I . . . I just feel so out of control. So . . . miserable."

"My life, too," Lucy whispered back. "Such a bad time. Me, too, Nicole. Me, too."

I let go of her and took a step back. I wiped the tears from my cheeks with both hands and stared at her in surprise. "You, too?" I choked out. "You're having a bad time, too?"

She nodded. Then her eyes flashed. Like green fire. "But I have an idea," she whispered. "I know what we can do."

"An idea?" I repeated, staring back at her. "Lucy, what kind of idea?"

Her eyes lit up again. Her face glowed with excitement. "Let's switch bodies," she said.

Don't miss these chilling tales from

FEAR STREET®

After hours, the horror continues at

FEAR STREET® NIGHTS

R.L. STINE

FEAR STREET®

SWITCHED

Simon Pulse
New York   London   Toronto   Sydney

A Parachute Press book

This book is a work of fiction. Any references to historical events, real people, or real locales are used fictitiously. Other names, characters, places, and incidents are the product of the author's imagination, and any resemblance to actual events or locales or persons, living or dead, is entirely coincidental.

SIMON PULSE
An imprint of Simon & Schuster Children's Publishing Division
1230 Avenue of the Americas, New York, NY 10020
Copyright © 1992 by Parachute Publishing, L.L.C.
All rights reserved, including the right of reproduction in whole or in part in any form.
SIMON PULSE and colophon are registered trademarks of Simon & Schuster, Inc.
FEAR STREET is a registered trademark of Parachute Press, Inc.
Designed by Sammy Yuen Jr.
The text of this book was set in Times.
Manufactured in the United States of America
This Simon Pulse edition April 2006
10 9 8 7
Library of Congress Control Number 2005929888
ISBN-13: 978-1-4169-1375-7
ISBN-10: 1-4169-1375-0

part one

The Switch

chapter

1

My name is Nicole Darwin and I'm a loser.

At least, that's the way I feel these days. Even the beautiful spring weather we've been having—the red and yellow tulips bobbing in the soft, warm breezes, the fresh smell of newly cut grass—can't cheer me up.

My life is the worst.

I tore a fingernail while getting dressed for school this morning and burst into tears. That's how messed up I am.

My fingernails are long and perfect. Sometimes I polish them rose red, sometimes a lilac purple. Some of the girls tease me about them. But I think they're pretty.

I don't know. I just like the way they look.

I think I'm pretty good looking. I'm not a knockout beauty or anything. But I'm okay. I have straight, dark brown hair, which I wear long, swept back over my shoulders. And I have really good skin, very creamy and pale.

Everyone tells me my eyes are my best feature. They're very light brown and very expressive. My boyfriend, David, says my eyes are mysterious. He says he can stare right into them and not have a single clue about what I'm thinking.

David is right about that. He usually doesn't have a clue about what I'm thinking.

He's a nice guy, but he mostly thinks about himself.

Besides, how could he know what I'm thinking? I always have such weird thoughts.

I wonder if everyone has weird thoughts like me.

Mom says I'd be beautiful if I'd smile more. She says that my hangdog expression pulls down my whole face.

She also thinks I should cut my hair short. "Why do you need so much hair?" she asks, shaking her head. Her hair is cropped nearly as short as a man's. "Think of all the hours you spend washing it and caring for it."

Mom is full of advice.

Sometimes she can be a real pain. She'll see that I'm unhappy, that I'm depressed about something. But that doesn't stop her from unloading more advice.

4

Does she really think I want to be just like her?

She and Dad are so boring. It's pitiful to watch them at the dinner table every night, struggling to think of something to say to each other.

When I get married, I hope I don't sit around talking about how hot it is outside and whether or not to buy a new kind of weed killer.

It's so depressing!

My parents are always in my face. I'm not the only one who notices it. My friends at Shadyside High agree with me. They all have a lot more freedom than I do.

They can take the car and drive around at night and visit friends and stuff. They don't have to tell their parents everywhere they're going and when they'll be back, the way I do.

After all, we're seniors. We're practically adults.

I don't see why I have to call and check in with my parents if I'm away more than a couple of hours or if I'm going to be later than I said.

I can take care of myself. They've got to learn to give me some space.

I could go on and on about Mom and Dad. But they're not the only reason I've been feeling really messed up these days.

I've had a few problems in school. I don't know if it's spring fever or what.

I should have written my biology report. But I didn't.

Mr. Frost made such a big deal of it. He made me feel like a criminal. Like I'd killed someone or something.

He called me in after school for one of our "private chats." That's what he calls them. He and I have had several "chats." But I don't know how you can call it a chat if it's just one person giving another person a hard time.

"You should have written your paper, Nicole." That's how Mr. Frost started the "chat."

I call him Frosty. Because he's big and round like a snowman.

"You should have written your paper, Nicole."

"I know," I replied, trying not to yawn in his face.

He waved a chubby hand, brushing away a fly that kept circling his face. First fly of spring, I thought.

"Why didn't you write it?" he demanded. He spoke in a soft, gentle voice that got softer the angrier he became.

I shrugged. "Don't know."

I really didn't know. I had planned to write it. I even did most of the research. I just never got around to it.

"You have to have some kind of excuse, Nicole," Frosty said, his voice growing even quieter.

I glanced out the window. The guys on the Tigers baseball team were doing warm up drills on the practice field. Clouds lifted away from the sun, and the room filled with light.

"I don't really have an excuse," I confessed.

We were both standing. He leaned his back against

6

the chalkboard behind his desk. I stood on the other side of the desk, my arms crossed.

I wore a black tank top and dark denim jeans. Black to match my mood.

The night before, I'd thought about painting my nails black. But I was on the phone for an hour with my best friend, Lucy Kramer, and I didn't get around to it.

"Well, what are we going to do about this?" Mr. Frost asked softly. "I don't want to fail you, Nicole. It would keep you from graduating."

Those words woke me up. *No way* I wasn't graduating this spring. I was counting the days till I was out of there.

"Uh . . . maybe I could hand it in late," I suggested. "It wouldn't take me long to write it, Mr. Frost. I've done all the research. Really."

I had been tugging tensely at a strand of dark brown hair. I brushed it back behind my shoulder.

Frosty pressed his lips together and gazed at me thoughtfully. He rubbed two or three of his chins.

"I've done all the work," I repeated. "Please let me write it. I know it'll be really good."

He kept me in suspense a few moments longer. Then he said, "If you hand it in Monday, I'll accept it."

"But today is Friday!" I blurted out.

"I know, Nicole. Spend the weekend on it. If I give you longer, it isn't fair to the others in the class. Do a good job. I'm counting on you."

He opened a notebook on his desk and started leafing through it. I took that to mean the "chat" was over.

I muttered "Thank you" and stomped from the classroom.

I felt really steamed. I guess I was more angry at myself than at Frosty. I mean, it wasn't his fault that I had messed up the assignment.

Nicole, why do you always make things so hard for yourself?

I couldn't answer my own question.

I'm going to have to work twenty hours a day to get that paper written, I told myself. That meant I had to tell David that I couldn't go to the dance club with him Saturday night.

This didn't make me happy at all.

David had been acting pretty weird lately. He had broken a couple of dates. He seemed sort of distant. As if he had something on his mind.

Which wasn't like David. He's a pretty laid-back, go-with-the-flow kind of guy. He's not an airhead or anything. He's just real easygoing.

Anyway, with David acting so strange, I really wanted to go out with him Saturday night. Maybe find out what was stressing him out. But there was no way I could go out Saturday night—*and* get the paper written.

To my surprise, David was waiting for me outside the science lab. "What are *you* doing here?" I greeted him.

"Waiting for you," he replied. David is a man of few words. He seldom says a whole sentence. He thinks it's kind of cute and appealing.

So do I.

I reached my face up to kiss him. He's very tall, nearly a foot taller than me.

He pulled back.

I gazed up at him. Tried to read his expression. He has these big, brown soulful puppy-dog eyes. He turned them away from me.

What's his problem? I wondered.

I decided I'd better just come right out and tell him that Saturday night was off.

But he beat me to it. "I . . . can't go out Saturday night," he said, still gazing down the empty hall.

"Excuse me? Why not?" I demanded, unable to hide my surprise.

He hesitated. We had been walking slowly side by side to my locker. But he stopped. He shoved his hands into his jeans pockets. "Just can't," he muttered.

"David, what's going on?" I asked, trying to keep my voice from getting too shrill. "What's happening Saturday night?"

He shrugged. "Made other plans," he said. His expression changed. Now he looked really embarrassed. "Listen, Nicole . . ."

I waited for him to go on. But he didn't.

I felt a stab of dread in my chest. I suddenly felt cold all over. "Are you . . . breaking up with me?" I asked.

The words didn't sound real. They didn't sound as if they were coming from me.

I had counted on David. Things had been tough for me. Real tough. I needed David. I needed him to keep me on a steady course.

I was so depressed. So low. I didn't need more bad news.

"Well? Are you?" I demanded.

He nodded. Those brown, soulful eyes locked on mine. "Yeah. I guess."

"But—*why?*" I cried. I couldn't keep my cool. I was just so shocked.

"It's too much," he replied.

Typical David answer. What did *that* mean?

I grabbed his arm. "I don't get it," I said. "At least tell me why, David. I really don't get it."

"It's just too much," he repeated.

I saw that my fingernails were digging into his skin. He pulled out of my grasp. He backed away.

"David—!" I cried.

"Listen, I'll call you later or something," he said. He started backing down the long hall. "Okay? Call you later. Sorry. Sorry, Nicole."

He turned and hurried away, taking long strides.

He didn't glance back.

I stood staring at him until he disappeared around the corner. A few seconds later I heard the front door to the school slam.

I realized I was trembling. I walked over to my locker and tried to open the combination lock. But my hand was shaking and my eyes were blurred with hot tears. I couldn't see the numbers.

Why didn't he explain? I wondered.

"It's just too much."

What did that mean? What was he trying to say?

After several tries I managed to unfasten the lock and pull the door open. I checked the calendar hanging on my locker door. I wanted to see if it was Friday the thirteenth.

No. It was the twelfth.

Still my unlucky day.

With a sigh I bent down and stuffed books and notebooks into my backpack. I couldn't really see what I was taking. I didn't care.

I have to get out of this building, I told myself.

If I don't, I'll suffocate. I really will.

I slammed the locker door shut, hoisted the backpack over one shoulder, and hurried down the hall. Two teachers came around the corner, laughing about something.

They stopped laughing when they saw me. I guess they caught the unhappy expression on my face.

"Nicole—are you okay?" one of them called.

"Yeah. Just fine!" I shouted. I pushed open the front door and stepped out of the school.

The air smelled fresh and sweet. A dogwood tree in front of the building was in full bloom, covered in dazzling white blossoms.

I turned my eyes to the street. A red and white Shadyside city bus pulled away from the corner. Two kids from the middle school whirled along the sidewalk on Rollerblades.

I didn't see anyone I knew. My friends had all gone home or to their after-school jobs by now.

Mom is probably wondering why I'm late, I thought bitterly. I could hear her voice now: "Nicole, if you knew you had to stay after school, why didn't you call and tell me?"

I have no life. No life at all!

I started down the steps when I saw Lucy coming toward me. She gave me a friendly wave. I hurried to greet her. Lucy and I have been best best best friends since we were in preschool.

Lucy has straight blond hair. But hers is shorter than mine, and she usually pulls it back in a ponytail. She has green eyes, a tiny, upturned nose, and a very sweet smile. I guess you'd say she was more cute than pretty.

I ran up to her and hugged her. I was suddenly overcome with emotion. "Lucy—it's been such a *horrible* day!" I blurted out. Hot tears ran down my cheeks.

Lucy was so understanding. So smart. And she knew me so well.

We had no secrets from each other. None at all. It was wonderful to have one special friend I could always trust.

"My life—it's all falling apart today," I told her. "Everything. I . . . I just feel so out of control. So . . . miserable."

"My life, too," Lucy whispered back. "Such a bad time. Me, too, Nicole. Me, too."

I let go of her and took a step back. I wiped the tears from my cheeks with both hands and stared at her in surprise. "You, too?" I choked out. "You're having a bad time, too?"

She nodded. Then her eyes flashed. Like green fire. "But I have an idea," she whispered. "I know what we can do."

"An idea?" I repeated, staring back at her. "Lucy, what kind of idea?"

Her eyes lit up again. Her face glowed with excitement. "Let's switch bodies," she said.

chapter

2

I followed Lucy to Fear Street. I felt a tingling excitement as we walked. I felt charged, as if an electrical current circled my body.

Was she serious? Did she mean it? Were we really going to switch bodies?

The ground grew dark, then light again as clouds rolled rapidly over the sky, blocking the sunlight, then allowing it to beam down again. The changing light gave everything an unreal feeling.

I told Lucy about my day, about my unhappiness. About David and Mr. Frost and the science report. About my parents, smothering me. Not letting me breathe.

She nodded, understanding. She didn't need to reply.

She wore a short black skirt over pale yellow tights. Her yellow sleeveless T-shirt revealed her slender, winter-pale arms.

Our shoes crackled over dry, dead leaves from the winter.

The sun faded and the old trees over Fear Street darkened. Then they flared brightly again, like someone turning the brightness control on the TV.

I shuddered as we stopped to stare up at the old Simon Fear mansion. I'd heard so many creepy stories about the burned-out old house, about this street.

"Why don't they just tear it down?" Lucy demanded, squinting through the now-bright sunlight. "It's such an eyesore!"

"Maybe they're afraid to," I replied in a hushed voice.

I gazed across the street at the old cemetery with its ancient, crooked gravestones jutting up from the ground like broken teeth.

Beyond the cemetery stretched the Fear Street woods. Ancient maple and birch trees, unfurling their fresh spring leaves, reached over the street, tangling together, like dozens of arms.

As I followed Lucy into the woods, the old trees formed a tall arch over our heads, nearly shutting out all the sunlight, covering the woods in grays and dark blues, dark as evening.

"Where are we going?" I asked breathlessly.

Lucy seemed to know the way. She kicked brambles away, leaning forward as she walked, following an invisible path.

"Lucy—wait up!" I called, stepping around a deep, marshy puddle. "Hey—Lucy! Wait!"

I caught up with her near a fallen, moss-covered tree. She stared down, and I followed her gaze. Thousands of tiny white insects swarmed over the green moss.

"Yuck," I murmured. "How gross."

Lucy nodded. She wiped her forehead with the back of her hand. It wasn't a really hot day, but we were both perspiring.

"Where are we going?" I repeated my question.

Lucy pointed past the fallen tree. "It's right up there. I think."

"What is?" I demanded. "Why are you being so mysterious?"

She grinned at me. "It's a mysterious place." She took my hand. My hand was cold. Hers felt hot and damp. "Stop asking so many questions," she scolded. "Follow me."

She tugged me over the moss-covered tree. I imagined the thousands of white insects crawling over me. The thought made me shudder.

"Are we really going to do it?" I asked her. "Are we really going to switch bodies?"

She narrowed her eyes at me. With that cute button nose and her delicate features, she looked twelve

16

instead of seventeen. "You *want* to do it—don't you?" she asked softly.

I nodded, thinking about my parents, my schoolwork, about David . . . about my messed-up life.

Yes. I wanted to get away. Get away from myself.

I wanted to get as far away from myself as I could. Yes. Yes.

Yes, I wanted to trade places with Lucy. I wanted to trade lives—for a while, anyway.

Lucy didn't have an easy life. Her parents battled like wild animals in a zoo. They were so wrapped up in their own problems, they hardly paid any attention to Lucy.

But I would like that, I decided. I'd like that a lot. Yes. Yes. Let's trade, I thought.

Lucy didn't have it easy. But her life was better than mine.

And she had Kent. Kent Borden was such a great guy. So smart. So funny.

Even though Lucy was my best friend, I'd often wondered what it would be like to go out with Kent. Kent instead of David.

Now I'll find out, I thought.

Lucy and I will switch bodies. And I'll find out what it's like to be with Kent.

Such sick, strange thoughts.

The light became grayer, the air heavier as we moved deeper into the woods. Our shoes crunched over the blanket of dead leaves that covered the ground.

"I think it's right up there," Lucy said, stopping to pull a white burr from her hair. "Ouch! It's prickly!" She tossed it to the ground.

A bird uttered a long, loud cry, somewhere above our heads. It was such a sad wail, it made me stop. "It sounds so human," I told Lucy. "Like a human crying."

The sound repeated. I hesitated, chilled by the strange, mournful sound.

Lucy's expression grew solemn. "Don't chicken out," she scolded. "Don't chicken out now. You want to do this, Nicole. You know you do."

I gazed at her, surprised by her sudden seriousness. "I'm coming with you," I said softly. "I'm not chickening out."

The bird wailed above our heads as we made our way through a tangle of scrub pine. Just beyond the shrubs stretched a long stone wall. Built of smooth gray stones, the wall reached a foot or so over our heads.

"My grandfather described this wall," Lucy confided. "Before he died, Grandpa told me where it was, told me the story of how it came to be built and how it got its incredible powers."

I swallowed hard, staring straight ahead at the wall. Deep cracks crisscrossed its surface like roads on a map. The plaster between the stones was chipped and broken.

"The wall is old, huh?" I asked my friend.

She nodded, staring straight ahead at it. "No one knows how old."

"And who built it?" I asked, brushing a mosquito off my arm.

"No one knows that, either. At least that's what Grandpa told me. He said it's called the Changing Wall. He said that over a hundred years ago, evil people came to the woods to use the wall and change their bodies. To switch bodies with unwilling victims."

I gasped. "You mean they *forced* people to change bodies with them?"

Lucy nodded. "That's how they escaped from paying for the crimes they had committed."

I stared at the wall. "Wow," I murmured. I turned to Lucy. "How did your grandfather find out about it?"

"From the old caretaker at the Fear Street cemetery," Lucy replied. "The caretaker lived in a cottage in the woods behind the cemetery. He knew all the old stories and legends—horror stories, mostly—of what went on in the woods. He would never repeat the stories, until one day many years ago. On that day, he told my grandfather the secret of the Changing Wall."

Lucy ran her hand gingerly over a smooth gray stone on the wall. As she touched it, the sky grew even darker. A deep gray settled around us. It seemed as if her touching the wall had made the world grow darker.

But of course that was only my twisted imagination.

I reached up my hand to touch the wall, but slowly drew it back.

Lucy snickered. "It's only stones and plaster, Nicole. It won't bite you."

"H-how does it work?" I stammered. My chest suddenly felt fluttery. I realized I was very frightened.

"Grandpa explained it all. It's really so simple," Lucy replied. "We climb up on the wall. We hold hands. We jump off, down to the other side. And when we land on the other side of the wall—"

"When we land, we're switched?" I interrupted.

Lucy nodded. "When we land, we will be switched. Your mind will be in my body. And my mind will be in your body. When people look at me, I'll look like you and everyone will think I'm you."

I stared at her, letting her words sink in. Then I raised my eyes to the wall, so gray and solemn, its dark shadow slanting over us.

"You really want to do this?" I asked Lucy.

"Come on. We have to try it," she replied. She took my hand again. This time both of our hands were cold and clammy.

She squeezed my hand. "It's so simple, Nicole. A simple jump. We have to try it. We really have to."

She raised her hands toward the top of the wall. "Give me a boost," she instructed.

I helped hoist her onto the top. It took her a short while to gain her balance. "It's kind of bumpy up here," she warned, lowering herself onto her knees.

"The wall is so narrow and cracked. Be careful, Nicole. Be careful not to fall off."

She reached down both hands to help pull me to the top.

I hesitated. Behind us I heard the mournful wail of the bird, high in the trees.

Was it a warning sound?

Was the bird warning me away?

What kind of a bird sounds so much like a girl crying so bitterly? I wondered.

"Come on, Nicole," Lucy urged, shaking her hands impatiently. "Hurry. It's hard to balance up here. And the stones are cutting my knees."

I ignored the wails of the bird and grabbed Lucy's hands. She tugged me to the top. I scraped my left knee on the side. But I managed to scramble up beside my friend.

On our knees we rested a few minutes, catching our breath.

Then we both slowly, carefully, climbed to our feet. And turned to face the other side.

I don't know why, but I expected to see something different on the other side of the wall. Different trees. Different sky. A house or something.

Some sign that everything on the other side was changed.

But the clearing on the other side was surrounded by the same tangled, shadowy woods.

My knees began to tremble as I took Lucy's hand. *Can I do this?* I asked myself. *Can I really do this?*

21

A simple jump, I reminded myself. That's all there is to it. A simple jump.

And my life will be changed.

Lucy and I glanced at each another. I could see my fear reflected in her dark green eyes. I was sure she could see her fear reflected in mine.

It was as if we had traded our frightened feelings even before we leapt off the wall together. As if the switch had already begun.

My chest fluttered so hard, I could barely breathe. Cold sweat trickled down my cheeks.

I grabbed Lucy's hand. I held it tightly.

I lowered my eyes to the ground. Not a very far jump. Onto tall, soft grass.

"Ready?" Lucy asked softly.

"Ready," I replied without hesitation.

I squeezed her hand. I took a deep breath.

And we both jumped.

chapter

3

I hit the ground hard, landing on both feet. Pain shot up from my ankles, and I dropped to my knees.

The pain roared up my legs, my chest, my head. The woods turned bright scarlet.

Breathing hard, I shook away the pain and climbed to my feet.

Had it worked? Had our jump to the other side of the wall made us change bodies?

I turned to Lucy—but she had disappeared. "Lucy?"

I was staring at *myself!*

Her mouth—*my* mouth dropped open as she stared back at me.

I lowered my eyes to examine myself. I was wearing Lucy's clothes—the sleeveless yellow T-shirt, the short black skirt over yellow tights.

"Oh, wow!" I murmured. I slid my hands over my face. Felt my nose. Lucy's tiny nose. Reached up and ran one hand over my ponytail. Lucy's hair. Not my hair.

I'm Lucy, I realized.

I'm Nicole in Lucy's body.

We were both giggling now. Both staring at each other, wide-eyed, not believing it. Staring and giggling.

Neither of us said anything.

We both started laughing hard. We tossed back our heads and laughed up at the sky.

I felt giddy. I felt crazy. I felt out of control.

Tears of laughter brimmed in my eyes. Through the tears, I stared at myself. At Lucy in my body. It wasn't like looking in a mirror. I realized I had never really seen myself before.

I had never seen the single dimple that deepened in my right cheek when I laughed. Never noticed that my mouth curled up more on one side than the other.

I had never been able to see how my long hair glistened down my back. How it swished behind me with each turn of my head.

It's so strange, so totally strange. I'm *outside* myself, I thought. I'm outside myself watching *me*.

I'm Lucy now, watching Nicole.

I stared as Nicole raised her hands to her cheeks, saw her long red nails spread out against her face.

We were still laughing, tears running down our cheeks.

And suddenly we were hugging each other, holding on to each other tightly. Laughing and hugging. Laughing and crying at the same time.

We started spinning. Holding on to each other, we started spinning in a wild, joyful dance.

Spinning faster and faster. Nicole and Lucy. Lucy and Nicole. Switched. Whirling together. Together. Not one. Not the other.

Spinning in a circle of both of us.

Whirling and laughing. So much joy.

And then it ended as sudden as the jump that started it. And we dropped to our knees on the warm grass, breathing hard. And gazed at each other with solemn expressions.

The giddiness vanished, and we realized what we had done.

We had jumped more than a few feet. We had jumped into new lives. Jumped into each other's life.

Lucy began singing. "Dum-dum-dum-dum dum-dum-dum-dum." I recognized the theme song from *The Twilight Zone.*

I laughed. "You're right," I agreed. "We've stepped into the Twilight Zone."

"We can't tell anyone," Lucy said, her voice a hushed whisper now. "Not anyone, Nicole."

"Call me Lucy," I told her. "I'm *you* now. Call me by your name."

She hesitated. "I still think of *myself* as Lucy," she said. "Even though I look like Nicole now."

"You're right," I agreed. "We can't tell anyone. No one would believe it anyway. We'll live each other's lives for a while—"

"And when we get tired of it," Lucy interrupted, "we'll come back here to the Changing Wall. And we'll change back."

"Yes," I quickly agreed. Then I felt a pang of guilt.

"What's wrong?" Lucy asked. She must have seen my expression change.

"I won't *want* to change back," I confessed. "My life is the pits. I—I think you made a bad deal, Lucy."

"Nicole, don't worry about it," she replied. "I think—"

"But my parents are so awful!" I cried. "They're like watchdogs. Always sniffing, always alert, always waiting to catch me in some kind of trouble. And . . . and David—"

"What about David?" Lucy asked softly.

"I told you he broke up with me," I replied. "So you won't have a boyfriend."

She smiled and brushed back her long, dark brown hair with the shiny red fingernails. "Maybe I'll try to win him back," she purred.

"And now I have Kent," I continued, still troubled and guilty. "Kent is such a great guy. How do you feel about that, Lucy? How do you feel about me going out with Kent now?"

She shrugged. "Nicole, this was my idea, remember? I knew exactly what I was getting into."

I opened my mouth to reply, but there didn't seem to be any more to say. The sky above the trees darkened. The afternoon sun had started to lower itself. A warm breeze made the newly unfurled leaves shimmer and whisper all around us.

"We'd better get home," Lucy said.

"My mom will be waiting for you at the door," I warned her. "You'd better have a good excuse ready."

"I'll just tell her we jumped off a wall and switched bodies, and that's why I'm late," Lucy said, grinning. My dimpled grin. She tossed back my dark brown hair as she started to laugh.

We both laughed. I still felt so giddy, so strange.

I stretched my arms above my head. I took a few steps over the tall grass in my new body.

I felt awkward. The legs moved differently. The feet were smaller. It took an effort to stand up straight, to keep the head raised.

Walking should be natural, I told myself. But I just wasn't used to this body.

A few more steps. I glanced back at the wall. In the fading light it appeared to be a gray blur. Just a dark cloud above the grass. If I didn't squint, I couldn't see it at all.

As if it didn't exist.

Lucy and I didn't say much as we made our way through the woods to the street. I guess we were lost in our own thoughts, thinking about our new lives. Getting used to our new bodies.

A few minutes later we stepped back onto Fear Street. The old Fear mansion rose up like a dark creature against the graying sky. I saw two scrawny cats scampering along a row of graves in the cemetery.

We walked on in silence. I said goodbye to Lucy about a block from my house. "Good luck!" I cried.

"Good luck," she echoed. Then she waved to me, turned, and jogged across the street.

I stood and stared. It was just so *weird* watching myself run away.

I watched Lucy until the trees blocked her from view. Then I turned and headed toward her house on Canyon Drive.

Can I really fool Lucy's parents? I wondered.

Can I really make the Kramers think that I'm their daughter?

And will I be able to fool Lucy's friends? Will I be able to fool Kent? Will I be able to fool my *own* friends?

So many questions as I hesitated at the bottom of Lucy's driveway and stared up at her little white shingled house.

Remember, Nicole—I warned myself—don't be sarcastic. Lucy is never sarcastic. *You're* the sarcastic one. Lucy is sweet and serious.

I took a deep breath and made my way up to the

house. The front door was open halfway. I pulled open the screen door and stepped into the small entryway.

"Hi! I'm home!" I called. "Sorry I'm so late!"

No reply.

The car was in the driveway. The Kramers had to be home.

"Where are you?" I called.

I started into the living room.

But stopped at the doorway with a loud gasp.

I blinked several times, but the gruesome scene refused to go away.

I grabbed the doorframe with both hands and stared down in horror at the dark puddles of blood. The slashed bodies sprawled on the floor.

And then I opened my mouth in a scream I thought would never end.

chapter
———————
4

My legs trembled so violently, I fell. Landed on my knees.

My whole body shuddered. I fought back the nausea that choked my throat.

Lucy's parents lay dead on the living room carpet. On their backs. Their bodies slashed and ripped. Their clothes cut and soaked with blood. Eyes staring blankly up at the ceiling in wide horror.

And the blood . . . The puddles . . . So dark and wide . . . beneath their cut, twisted bodies like wine-colored rafts.

Like deep, dark holes in the shaggy white rug.

The Kramers. Lucy's parents. Murdered. Dead on the living room floor.

"Lucy. Lucy. Lucy." I don't know how long I repeated her name.

I don't know how long I remained there at the living room doorway, on my knees, trembling all over, blinking rapidly, staring at the horror.

Staring at the slashed bodies of Lucy's parents.

Repeating my friend's name in a low chant. "Lucy. Lucy. Lucy."

I could have been there for only a minute or two. Or it could have been an hour.

"Lucy. Lucy. Lucy."

Waves of red rushed before my eyes. Hot waves of red blood washed over me, blinding me, choking me.

"Lucy. Lucy. Lucy."

Rubbing my eyes, trying to rub away the ugly scene of horror, I struggled to my feet.

And staggered to the front door.

"Got to tell Lucy," I murmured out loud.

I couldn't think of anything else. The horror was too fresh, the blood too red.

"Got to tell Lucy."

I stumbled out the front door. My new body still felt strange. I had to concentrate on placing one foot in front of the other.

Lucy and I will have to switch back now, I realized. We'll have to return to that gray wall in the woods and switch back.

Poor Lucy.

She wanted to try a new life. But now . . .

Every time I blinked, I saw the dark puddles on the

white carpet, saw the Kramers' blank, staring eyes. Saw their clothes all cut . . . all cut . . .

Somehow I made it to my house. My ponytail had come undone, but I made no attempt to fix it. I had torn the yellow tights.

The sun had lowered behind the houses, cooling the air. But I was drenched in sweat.

I must have run the whole way. At least six blocks. I didn't remember running. But I was gasping for air, my chest heaving up and down, as I crossed the street to my house.

Over the front lawn. The grass freshly mowed. Moist blades sticking to my sneakers as I ran.

Onto the front porch. "Lucy! Lucy!" My voice breathless and shrill as I frantically called her name.

I stopped outside the front door. Stopped to catch my breath. And to think.

How could I tell her what I had seen in her living room?

How could I tell her?

How?

chapter

_____

5

I'll have to get her alone, I decided.

My parents will think I'm Lucy. They'll wonder why I am bursting in at dinnertime. They'll wonder why my hair is all disheveled and my clothes torn. They'll wonder why I am so upset and out of breath.

There will be so many questions, questions, questions.

I'll drag Lucy outside. And then . . . I'll tell her there's been an accident.

Yes, an accident, I decided.

I won't break it to her all at once. I'll be careful and considerate. I won't just blurt out that her parents have both been murdered in their living room.

I won't tell her about the blood . . . the blood . . . the blood . . .

I swallowed hard. Cupped my hand over my mouth as I started to retch.

I couldn't hold it back any longer. The horror I had seen was too overwhelming.

Bending over at the bottom of the driveway, I vomited until my sides ached. My stomach heaved again and again, as if my whole body was trying to push away what I had seen.

My legs trembling, I sucked in one deep breath after another, uttering low moans, waiting for my stomach to stop lurching.

When I finally felt a little steadier, I made my way to the front door. I turned the knob.

Locked.

I started to call out, "Lucy!" But I stopped myself, remembering that she was Nicole now.

I rang the bell. I heard it chime once, twice, three times inside my house.

No reply.

I stumbled off the front stoop and made my way around to the back. The kitchen door was locked, too. Even though it was dinnertime, the kitchen stood dark and empty.

I knocked loudly on the kitchen door. "Anyone home? Nicole—are you here?" I called.

Silence.

I pressed my forehead against the glass on the door and peered in again.

No one home, I realized.

Where were they? Had they gone out for dinner?

"Lucy, where are you?" I whispered. "Lucy, you have to know what happened. I have to tell you, Lucy. I have to tell *someone.*"

I couldn't keep it to myself much longer. I couldn't hold the horror in without exploding. Without going totally crazy.

I backed away from the kitchen door, my hands pressed to my face. I expected to feel my long, red nails pushing against my skin. But, of course, I didn't have my nails. I had Lucy's short, chewed-up nails.

Picturing the Kramers on their living room rug, I began to feel the waves of nausea again. I knew there was nothing left to vomit up.

My mind spun wildly. Who can I tell? Who?

The Shadyside police?

How could I tell the police before I told Lucy? How could I tell them before we switched back into our own bodies?

No, I decided. It would be too confusing. Too confusing and painful for all of us.

I won't tell the police until I've told Lucy, I told myself.

And then Kent's face flashed into my mind.

Kent. He was so smart and kind. So thoughtful. So understanding.

Kent will listen to me, I decided. Kent will believe me.

Kent will help me.

I swallowed hard, struggled to catch my breath, to stop my legs from shaking. I pushed back the moist strands of blond hair that had fallen across my forehead.

Yes. Kent.

Kent's house was only two blocks away. I jogged down the driveway, glancing back at my house, so dark and empty.

Two boys raced by on bikes as I reached the sidewalk. I didn't see them until they were practically on top of me.

"Look out!" I heard one of them shout.

I saw them swerve to avoid hitting me.

"What's your problem?" the other boy shouted back.

If only he knew, I thought sadly.

I felt too strange, too upset to run. My heart fluttered in my chest like a dozen butterflies. My legs felt so heavy, as if I weighed a thousand pounds.

I walked through someone's flower garden. The wet dirt clung to my shoes. I nearly tripped over a blue skateboard someone had left at the bottom of their front yard.

The two blocks to Kent's house seemed a mile long. Finally I found myself staring up at the square, two-story redbrick house with its slanting, red tile roof.

Behind me on the street a car rolled past slowly. Its headlights swept over me. I realized I must look like a mess. Like a crazed wild person.

You can't worry about that now, I scolded myself.

If only I had been in my real body!

Would that have made me feel any better?

Probably not.

I didn't remember climbing the sloping lawn to Kent's front door. But here I was, pounding hard on the door with my fist, shouting Kent's name at the top of my lungs.

Be home! Be home! I silently prayed.

Someone has to be home tonight. *Someone* has to share this nightmare with me. *Someone* has to help me.

The porch light flashed on, casting a cone of yellow light over the front stoop. As I blinked against the sudden brightness, the front door swung open.

Kent poked his head out, his face pale in the porch light, his blue eyes wide with surprise.

"Please—help me," I stammered.

His eyes studied me, locked on to my eyes. "What's wrong?" he demanded.

I gazed past him, into the house. "Are your parents home?"

He shook his head. "No. They're in Waynesbridge. Why? What's the matter?"

I could feel the tears welling in my eyes, could feel the sobs building in my chest.

Nicole, don't cry! I instructed myself. You've got to get the story out. Don't cry. Don't cry now.

Save the tears for later.

You'll have plenty of time to cry when Lucy knows

37

what has happened and you are back in your own body.

"What's wrong?" Kent demanded. "You look terrible!"

"Can I come in?" My voice trembled. A single teardrop slid down my right cheek.

He stepped back and I pushed past him into the front room. I grabbed on to the back of the couch, squeezing the soft leather, holding myself up.

He followed me into the room, his handsome face tight with concern. He had straw-colored hair, wavy and thick, down over his collar. He had blue-gray eyes, serious eyes. He was tall and athletic looking.

I'd always admired him because he seemed so comfortable with himself. I don't think I ever saw him nervous or in a bad mood.

Now he narrowed his eyes at me, waiting for me to explain.

I glanced around, unsure of how to start. I saw a single place set at the dining room table. The house smelled of tomato sauce.

"Sit down and tell me what happened. I put a frozen pizza in the oven," Kent explained. "Did you eat yet?"

And then it all burst out of me in a flood of words. I started at the beginning—when I met Lucy after school—and told him everything.

"Lucy took me to Fear Street," I explained. "Her grandfather told her about the Changing Wall. We switched bodies, Kent. We both wanted to, and we did it."

His mouth dropped open. He raised a hand as a signal for me to stop.

But I couldn't stop. Not until I had revealed everything. "We switched bodies," I repeated. "I know it's hard to believe. But you have to. You *have* to. I know I look like Lucy, but I'm really Nicole."

"Listen, Nicole—" he started.

But I wouldn't let him talk. "Lucy went to my house, and I went to hers," I continued, talking fast, faster than I had ever talked in my life. "But when I got to her house . . . when I got to her house . . ."

"What?" Kent demanded impatiently. "What happened?"

"Oh, Kent!" I cried, letting the tears flow now. "Oh, Kent, it was so horrible! Both of her parents! Both of them were murdered. Slashed to pieces. I found their bodies on the living room floor. And I ran out. I've got to tell Lucy. I've got to. But she wasn't home. She wasn't at my house. She doesn't know, Kent. She doesn't know. I—I—"

The sobs leaped from my throat. My shoulders heaved up and down as I started to weep.

I felt Kent's hands on my shoulders, tenderly, trying to calm me. He held me and brought his face close to mine to whisper in my ear. "It's okay, Nicole. It's going to be okay."

I struggled to stop sobbing.

He was being so gentle, so kind. I knew he would be. He was such a good guy.

"Nicole, I'll help you," he said softly. "Don't worry. I'm going to help you."

He led me around to the front of the couch and helped me lower myself onto the cushion. Then he stayed with one hand on my shoulder, talking to me softly until I finally stopped crying.

"Thanks, Kent," I murmured, wiping my soggy cheeks with both hands. "Thanks."

"I'm going to get you some water to drink," he said, stepping away from the couch. "Don't get up, okay? Just stay right there."

"Okay," I replied. I thanked him again. I took deep breaths, trying to calm myself.

"Be right back," Kent said. He stepped through the dining room and disappeared into the kitchen.

A few seconds later I heard his voice from the kitchen.

Who is he talking to? I wondered.

I pushed myself to my feet and crept to the dining room on trembling legs. Halfway through the dining room, I could hear Kent's voice clearly. I realized he was on the phone.

"That's right, Officer," I heard him say, "I'm keeping her right here. But you'd better hurry. She might try to get away."

chapter
____

6

A silent gasp escaped my throat.

The room tilted in front of me. The floor rose up, and I had to grab the dining room table to steady myself.

I felt so betrayed. So confused and betrayed.

Why did Kent call the police? Didn't he believe my story?

Did he think I murdered the Kramers?

I heard him hang up the phone. Then I heard him walk to the sink. I heard the splash of water in the sink.

He was getting me the glass of water he had promised.

I hesitated, still holding on to the table edge, still waiting for the room to stop tilting and swaying.

What should I do?

There's no way I'm going to sit here and wait for the police, I told myself. Not in Lucy's body.

Unless I get back in my own body, no one will believe my story, I decided.

Kent had just pretended to believe me. Kent must think I'm Lucy. He only called me Nicole to humor me, to calm me down. So he could sneak into the kitchen and call the police at his first opportunity.

I could hear him shut off the water tap. I heard him open the freezer. Heard the *plop* of ice cubes dropping into the glass.

I took a step back. Then another. Moving back toward the living room.

I'm getting out, I decided. I'm not waiting around here.

Kent betrayed me. I'm not sure why.

"Hey, Nicole—how are you doing?" he called from the kitchen.

His cheerful voice made my skin crawl.

I'd always thought he was such a great guy. So smart and caring.

Now I hated him. Hated him for lying to me, for trying to trick me.

Hated him for not being my friend.

I turned and started to run. The room tilted and rose up, as if trying to keep me prisoner.

42

But I forced myself to run straight. Burst into the front hallway.

"Nicole—wait! Hey—Nicole!" I heard Kent's desperate shout behind me from the dining room.

I hit the screen door hard with my shoulder and bolted out of the house. I leaped down all three steps of the front stoop, and kept running.

"Hey, Nicole—stop! Come back!"

Was he going to chase after me?

I darted across the street, into someone's yard. Ducked low behind their tall evergreen hedge. Kept moving. Ignoring the pounding of my heart, the flashes of red, the images of the bloodred puddles that flared up every time I blinked.

I crossed another three or four yards before I dared to glance back. No sign of Kent. No. He wasn't coming after me.

"What's your problem, Kent?" I asked out loud, through gasps for breath. "What's your problem? Why did you do that to me? Lucy is your girlfriend, remember? Why did you call the police to come get your girlfriend?"

Cupping a hand over my ear, I listened for police sirens.

I didn't hear any. Somewhere down the block, two little kids were having a shrill argument.

"Did not!"

"Did, too!"

"Did not!"

Hearing their innocent voices made my breath catch in my throat. I suddenly wanted to be a little kid again. I didn't want to be Lucy anymore. I didn't want to be seventeen. I didn't want to know there were two slashed bodies lying on Lucy's living room floor.

I kept moving through front yards, crossing streets carefully, alert for the police. Alert for anyone who might be following me. Alert to every sound, every movement.

Lucy, I have to find you, I thought.

Lucy, I have such terrible news.

Without realizing it, I had returned to my house. I slipped across the driveway and clung to the wide trunk of the old sassafras tree near the walk.

The tree was an old friend. How many hours had I spent reading in its shade or playing around it with the neighborhood kids?

Holding on to the trunk, I gazed up at the house. Still dark and empty.

Lucy, where are you? Lucy, I need you.

I scratched my knee. Realized the tights were completely ripped. I swept my hair off my forehead. It felt wet and tangled.

I must look like a horror, I realized.

I heard voices. The neighbors stepping out of their house. I pressed against the tree, trying to hide myself.

I can't stay here, I realized. I can't stand here staring up at an empty house.

My mind whirred and spun, like a cyclone. I

pressed both hands against my temples, trying to force my thoughts to calm.

I'll go back to Lucy's house, I decided.

The neighbors' car started up. The sound made me jump. I pressed myself tighter against the friendly, old tree trunk. And waited for them to leave.

Their headlights swept over my yard, rolled down the tree trunk. Can they see me here? I wondered.

They didn't stop. I watched the car roll down the dark street.

Back to Lucy's house, I told myself. To change into fresh clothes. And fix my hair. And make myself look more together.

I'll rush past the living room.

I won't look in there again.

I don't need to see the Kramers' bodies again. I see them every time I shut my eyes.

I'll clean myself up. It'll make me feel a little better. And then I'll phone my house. I'll phone my house, and keep phoning until I reach Lucy.

I won't tell her the awful news over the phone. That would be too cruel, I decided. I can't do that to poor Lucy.

I'll tell her to meet me in the Fear Street woods. I'll tell her we have to switch back into our own bodies right way. Then when we've switched back, I'll tell her what has happened.

And I'll help her. I'll be there for her.

She's always been there for me.

Having a plan helped to calm me down a little. My heart still thudded in my chest. But the spinning, whirring cyclone of my thoughts slowed. And the ground stopped tilting as I walked.

As I turned the corner onto Canyon Drive, I heard the wail of sirens. Distant sirens. I stopped and listened. Were they coming this way? Were they coming for me?

The sound faded. Replaced by the soft whisper of the trees.

I ran the rest of the way to Lucy's house. Let myself in through the back door so I wouldn't have to go past the living room.

I clicked on the kitchen light and glanced around. The kitchen gleamed, clean and orderly. No sign that two horrible murders had taken place in the next room.

I shuddered and made my way to Lucy's room. It was at the end of a short hall on the first floor.

The hallway was dark. I fumbled along the wall, but couldn't find the light switch.

I bumped hard into something solid against the wall. It took me a few seconds to realize it was a wicker clothes hamper.

I stepped around it, rubbing my knee, and pushed open the door to Lucy's room. I waited for my eyes to adjust to the dim light from the window. Then I clicked on a small nightstand lamp.

It cast pale yellow light over the bed. My eyes swept over the smooth bedspread. To the closet.

I came back here to change, I remembered. I edged around the bed to the closet. Lucy's closet. Lucy's clothes.

The sliding door caught. It seemed to be off its track. I needed both hands to slide it open.

"Oh!" I uttered a cry as I stared into the closet.

Empty.

No clothes.

Two large cardboard cartons on the floor.

How can the closet be empty? Where are Lucy's clothes?

My heart thudded harder. I suddenly felt chilled.

What's going on here?

I spun away from the closet, lurched to the dresser against the wall, and began pulling open drawers.

Empty.

All empty.

Why would Lucy take all of her clothes? The question repeated in my mind.

Before I could answer it, I saw the blood-smeared knife on the desk.

And all questions and thoughts flew from my mind.

part two

The Murderer

chapter

7

The knife blade glowed dully in the yellow lamplight.

Dark purple stains ran down the blade, onto the desktop. Rivulets of dried blood.

I stared at the knife until it blurred before my eyes.

It isn't real, I thought.

I'm not staring at a blood-caked knife on Lucy's desk. I'm not. I'm *not!*

I tried to blink it away. But it would not leave.

It was real. A real knife. A kitchen knife. A black-handled kitchen knife.

I took a deep breath, then another. Then I made my way closer to the desk.

The knife stood upright. The blade had been plunged into the desk.

As I drew closer, I saw that the handle was also streaked with blood.

Such a big knife, I thought.

Such a big knife, all covered in blood.

Why is it here? Why is it sticking up from the desk in Lucy's room?

My hands pressed tightly against the sides of my face, I took another step closer.

The blade had been stabbed through a sheet of paper. A sheet of lined notebook paper.

A dark thumbprint smudged the bottom of the page. The thumbprint was dark purple. A thumbprint made of blood.

Struggling to focus my eyes, I saw writing on the paper. Scrawled handwriting in dark blue ink. Three lines of writing above the spot where the knife punctured the paper.

Squinting in the hazy light, I leaned close to the desk and read the scrawled words:

> I HAD TO KILL THEM
> I COULDN'T TAKE IT ANYMORE
> LUCY K

I swallowed hard. I had to force myself to breathe. "No!" I cried, backing away. "No! Please—no!"

I backed up until I reached the bed. Then I dropped

onto the smooth bedspread and buried my head in my hands.

I shut my eyes tight, but I could still see the scrawled words in my mind.

The scrawled confession. Lucy's confession.

She had murdered both of her parents. Stabbed them. Slashed them. Then plunged the murder weapon into the desk.

And then . . .

And then . . .

She took all of her clothes? Escaped with all of her clothes?

No. That made no sense.

I opened my eyes. Glanced up. Caught a glimpse of myself in the dresser mirror.

That glimpse made me realize the full horror. That one-second glimpse made everything come clear.

Lucy had murdered her parents. She wrote her confession. Left the murder weapon in her room for all to see.

Then she switched bodies with me!

Now here I sat. Lucy. I was Lucy.

I was the murderer!

And Lucy had escaped by becoming Nicole.

Lucy escaped by becoming me. And I became the murderer.

Oh, how cold! I realized. How cold, Lucy!

How did you ever plan something so cold?

The perfect crime. The perfect escape.

53

You are now Nicole. And no one will believe that I am not Lucy.

When I tell the truth, no one will believe me. Because I am Lucy the murderer.

No wonder Lucy was so eager to switch bodies with me, so eager to enter my unhappy, depressing life. She knew exactly what she was doing. She knew she was leaving me to take the blame. The blame for two horrible murders.

She knew she was making a clean escape.

Escape.

The word rang in my ears.

Escape. How can I escape?

I had a sudden impulse to grab the sheet of paper, to tear up the confession. To pull out the knife and hide it.

Then another frantic thought: I'll take the knife. I'll take the knife and find Lucy. I'll threaten her with it. I'll *force* her to switch bodies again.

I'll force her to let me be Nicole again.

If she won't, I told myself, I'll kill her! I really will! No. No. No.

I knew I couldn't kill anyone.

And I couldn't kill Lucy, even after what she had done to me.

But what could I do?

I have to find her, I decided. I have to talk to her. I have to—

My wild, unhappy thoughts were interrupted by a loud noise.

Startled, I leaped up off the bed.

A pounding. It repeated. Three knocks.

Someone at the front door?

I clicked off the bedside lamp, casting the room in darkness. Then I made my way past the desk, past the knife, past the handwritten confession.

I crept into the living room and pulled back the curtains just an inch. Stared out at the front stoop.

And saw two grim-faced men in gray suits.

Two police detectives.

chapter

8

"No way!" I whispered.

No way I was going to stay there and let them catch me. They weren't wearing uniforms, but I could tell they were police officers. I knew they were after me.

Seeing the two detectives made me forget my fright. A flood of anger rolled over me, sweeping my fear away.

I pushed the curtain back in place and edged away from the window. "No way," I whispered again.

I'm going to find Lucy, I decided. I'm not going to make this easy for her.

I'm not going to stand here beside the knife and the handwritten confession and say, "Here I am, officers. Take me away."

SWITCHED

I heard the insistent pounding on the front door.

I turned and hurried back along the short hallway, avoiding the clothes hamper this time.

My chest felt fluttery. But my mind was alert, alert to every sound, alert to every sight, every shadow.

I stepped into the kitchen. I had left the light on. I ducked low to keep from being seen through the window. Keeping my head down, I grabbed the back door by the knob and pulled it open.

The screen door rattled as I pushed it.

Had the police officers heard?

Were they coming around the back?

I slid out and carefully, silently closed the screen door behind me.

I glanced to the driveway, but I couldn't see anything. I listened hard for footsteps or voices.

Silence.

I'm out of here! I told myself. Taking a deep breath, I began jogging across the backyard.

A hazy half moon shimmered above the trees. The air was hot and very still.

My sneakers slipped and squeaked on the dew-wet grass. I was in the middle of the yard, past the small vegetable garden, almost to the rusted old swingset, when I heard a man's shout behind me.

"Hey—stop!"

I uttered a low cry and glanced back.

Both policemen were at the side of the house. One of them pointed to me. The other waved his hands above his head as if signaling.

"Stop! Don't move!"

"Stop right there!"

They sounded more surprised than angry.

I ignored their cries. Lowering my head, leaning forward, I ran full speed. Past the swingset. Between two tall maple trees that had once held a hammock. Past a low pile of fireplace logs.

"Stop! Hey—stop!"

I turned back to see that they were chasing after me, running fast, their hands swinging at their sides.

"Stop—!"

With a gasp I tried to pick up speed.

But the tall wooden fence rose up in front of me.

The tall wooden fence the Kramers had built at the back of their yard. The fence Lucy and I had helped to paint white. The fence where we had spent hour after hour bouncing a tennis ball and catching it.

The fence rose up in front of me like a prison wall.

And I knew that I was caught.

chapter

9

I raised both arms and grabbed at the fence. Jumped.

I had a crazy idea that I could climb over it.

But the fence was at least eight feet tall, the top out of my reach.

I could hear the two gray-suited police officers shouting behind me. I could hear their shoes thudding the ground.

With a loud groan I made another frantic jump, my hands stretched up as far as I could reach.

No. No way.

"Stop! Don't move!" the voice behind me commanded.

But you don't understand! I thought. *I'm not Lucy. I only look like Lucy.*

The fence glowed dully in the pale light of the half-moon. I took a deep breath, preparing to turn around, to face them and tell them who I really was.

But then I remembered the trick boards. The little doorway Lucy's dad had built for us. We thought it was so cool. The boards tilted back when we pushed them, and we scampered through the narrow opening like puppy dogs.

Was the doorway still there?

Lucy and I hadn't played with it since we were six or seven.

"Stop! We won't hurt you!"

"We want to help you!"

Liars. The voices snapped me out of my paralysis.

I dived at the fence.

Which boards? Which ones?

It had been so many years. I didn't remember.

I lowered my shoulder and pushed. No. Not there.

I let out a frightened cry. The cry of a trapped animal.

I tried again. Shoved my whole body against the boards to my right.

I heard a cracking sound. Then they gave way slowly. Two boards tilted up.

And I stumbled through the slender opening. Caught my balance. And kept running.

Through a dark alleyway. Past a row of metal trash cans.

Into someone's backyard.

I could hear the surprised shouts of the two officers. Then I could hear their shoes pounding the alleyway. They had squeezed through the same opening in the fence.

They were still close behind.

I can't outrun them, I realized. I can't run much farther.

Breathing hard, I let my eyes sweep over the backyard. A hiding place, I thought. There's got to be a hiding place.

My eyes stopped at a small shed near the house.

No. Not a shed. A little house with a slanting roof. A doghouse? A playhouse for kids?

My sneakers slipped on the dew-wet grass as I hurtled myself to the little house. I heard the two men at the back of the yard.

I plunged into the little house. Dropped to my knees and crawled inside. Then I tucked myself into a tight ball. Shut my eyes tight. Buried my head in my arms.

Like a little kid pretending she's invisible.

If I can't see you, then you can't see me.

I buried my head, held my breath. And prayed they hadn't seen me dive into this hiding place.

Over the pounding of my heart, I listened. Listened for their footsteps, their cries. Listened for them to run past, to keep running, to the next yard and the next.

Listened for them to admit they had lost me. To give up the search.

My heart nearly stopped when I heard one of them shout: "Over there!"

chapter
10

I let out a silent gasp. But I didn't move.

I stayed tucked in a tight ball, my head buried in my arms, my eyes shut tight.

No, you didn't see me, I thought, praying hard. *You can't see me. I'm invisible.*

"Where? Where'd she go?" The man's voice sounded breathless, desperate. I heard him start to cough, a long, wheezing cough.

"Next yard," his partner replied. "I think I saw her go around that garage."

"Take the front. I'll try the back." More coughing.

Then silence.

Yes. Yes.

I wanted to cry out, to leap out of the little house and jump for joy.

But I stayed wrapped up tightly, holding on to myself, holding myself together.

I don't know how long I remained curled up like that. It might have been only a few seconds. It might have been an hour.

I stayed until my body stopped trembling. Until my head stopped throbbing. Until the red flashes before my eyes dimmed to black.

I stayed until the silence became too loud to bear.

And when I climbed out of the little house, stretching my cramped muscles, raising my hands high over my head, I had a plan.

My car waited for me in the student parking lot behind the high school. My little red Civic. The only car in the narrow asphalt lot.

I had forgotten about it after school. In my excitement of following Lucy to the woods to switch bodies, I had completely forgotten that I had driven to school.

Was that really this afternoon? I asked myself.

It seemed as if it had happened days and days ago.

This has been the longest day of my life, I told myself. And the saddest.

My eyes darted over the empty parking lot. For some reason I felt like a criminal. Stealing my own car.

I usually kept my car keys in my jeans pocket. But I was wearing Lucy's clothes. Luckily, I kept a spare key hidden in one of those little magnetic cases under the fender.

I pulled open the door and slid behind the wheel.

I glanced tensely into the rearview mirror. I expected the two police officers to jump out from behind the school building.

But there was no one around.

My hand trembled as I slid the key into the ignition and started up the car. The hum of the engine sounded soothing. I sat there for a while, listening to the car, running my hands over the cool steering wheel.

"Lucy, I'm coming," I said out loud. "I'm going to find you now, Lucy. You won't get away."

I felt a little better, a little calmer, a little more confident as I switched on the headlights, then backed the little car out of the parking space.

A few seconds later I had eased past the side of the school and turned sharply onto Park Drive. A bright spotlight on the front of the school building cast a white cone of light over the bare flagpole. I caught a glimpse of a maroon and white banner, proclaiming GO, TIGERS! over the front doors.

I'm going to drive around town till I find Lucy, I vowed to myself. I'll drive to all of her hangouts. I'll drive everywhere she's ever been.

I won't give up. I'll find her. I'll get my real body back.

And I'll force her to tell me why she tricked me like this.

"Lucy, I thought you were my friend," I murmured out loud, easing through a stop sign. "How could you hate me so much? How could you hate me enough to want me to take the blame for your parents' murders?"

As I drove to my house, I tried to think back. Tried to think of something I had said to her, something I had done to her to make Lucy hate me.

But I drew a blank. I couldn't think of a thing.

We had always been so close. So honest with each other. If one of us was angry, we would tell the other. We would never keep it inside.

The dark houses and lawns whirred past in a blur of blacks and grays. I gripped the wheel tightly in both hands. It felt so solid, so real. I gripped it as if holding on to the real world. I had the strong feeling that if I let go of the wheel, I'd slip away, slip out of the car, into a dark, unreal world and be lost forever.

I cut the lights as I pulled to the curb in front of my house. If Lucy was home, I didn't want her to see me coming. I wanted to surprise her.

But I saw no car in the driveway. The porchlight was on, and the spotlight over the front lawn. My parents always left those lights on when they were away.

"Where are you?" I murmured out loud, peering at the dark windows. "Where are you this late at night? Lucy, I need my body back."

I suddenly found myself wondering if Lucy had been able to fool my parents. Did they think she was

Nicole? Did they think that I was with them? That nothing had changed?

I clicked on the headlights and eased away from the curb.

I'm not going to sit here, asking questions I can't answer, I told myself. I'm going to drive until I find Lucy.

I cruised through town, gripping the wheel tightly. Wherever I drove, Lucy's face floated in the windshield in front of me.

I'll find you. I'll find you. I'll find you. The vow became a chant in my mind.

I tried friends' houses without success.

I drove past my house a second time. A third time. Still dark.

I tried Alma's Coffee Shop, a little place where she sometimes hung out. No sign of her.

Each time I failed, I grew a little calmer, a little angrier, a little stronger and more determined to find her.

When I finally did track her down, I was ready.

She was sitting in a booth at the back of Pete's Pizza, a favorite hangout for Shadyside High kids at the Division Street Mall.

I had spotted her through the glass doors.

I stopped and stared. Stared at my body, sitting there with two other girls. Lucy in my body, talking and laughing, as if nothing terrible had happened.

I recognized Margie Bendell and Hannah Franks

sitting across from Lucy. They were all playfully tugging at a slice of pizza, the last piece on the tray. Lucy plucked off the top layer of cheese and tossed it at Margie.

I don't believe this! I thought, leaning against the glass doorway, staring at the three of them, staring at Lucy in my body.

Lucy laughing. Lucy having a great time.

While I lived a nightmare.

While I lived the nightmare she had created.

I could feel the anger flood my body, until I felt that I might explode into a million pieces. I grabbed the restaurant door, shoved it open, and stormed inside.

A waitress flashed me a startled look as I bumped her from behind and kept moving. "Excuse *me!*" she shouted sarcastically.

I barely heard her. My eyes were on Lucy. Lucy in my body. Lucy laughing with Margie and Hannah as she tore off a section of the pizza slice and stuffed it into her mouth.

I strode past a table of other kids I knew from school. One of them called out "Hi!" but I didn't reply.

Margie and Hannah sat across from each other. Margie turned as I stepped up to the booth. "Nicole! Hi!" she cried in surprise.

How does she know I'm Nicole? I asked myself.

I quickly answered my own question. *Lucy told her. Lucy told that we switched bodies.*

Margie and Hannah both know.

Just another broken promise of Lucy's. Just another lie she told me.

But why? I wondered. Why did Lucy tell them?

Lucy is a murderer. Why would she want these two girls to know that she isn't really Nicole? Why would she want them to know that she's hiding in my body?

"Nicole—what's up?" Hannah asked, tossing her cornrow braids behind her shoulders. She flashed me a smile. But the smile faded as she caught my troubled expression.

"Nicole—are you okay?" Margie demanded.

"No. No. I'm not okay," I told her. "I—I have to talk to Lucy."

Both girls gaped at me in surprise.

"But Lucy isn't here!" Margie declared.

I turned to Lucy's seat.

She was gone.

chapter

11

"Where—where did she go?" I stammered.

Hannah twirled the wrapper from a straw between her fingers. She gazed at Margie, then narrowed her hazel eyes at me. "Lucy? She wasn't here, Nicole."

"I saw her," I replied sharply.

Margie patted the cushion next to her. "Sit down, Nicole. Are you okay?"

"Lucy was here," I insisted, ignoring Margie's request. "I saw her when I came in. The three of you . . . you were arguing over the last slice."

I glanced down at the pizza tin. Empty except for a wedge of crust.

"No," Margie insisted softly. "It's just Hannah and me."

"You let her get away!" I cried shrilly.

"Nicole—please. Sit down," Margie insisted.

Margie and Hannah were in this together, I realized. Lucy had told them about our switching bodies. Now they were protecting her. They distracted me and allowed Lucy to slip away.

But why were they helping her? I wondered. They were my friends, too.

I crossed my arms tightly in front of me, to hold myself in, to keep myself from exploding. "I *know* you talked to Lucy!" I cried angrily. "If you didn't talk to her, how do you know that I'm Nicole?"

They both gaped at me. Hannah's mouth dropped open.

They couldn't answer the question. I had caught them in their lie.

"Nicole—" Margie started. She stepped out of the booth and tried to grab me.

But I was too fast for her. I spun away and started jogging down the long aisle to the door. "I know she's here. I'm going to find her!" I shouted back.

I heard Margie call my name. But I ducked around a group of tough-looking guys in muscle shirts and black denims who were entering the restaurant—and dived out the door.

Lucy is here and she couldn't have gone far, I told myself.

I crossed the mall walkway to the CD store and peered up and down. It was late, I realized. Several of the stores were closing for the night. Lights were dimming. Salespeople were locking doors.

The mall was nearly deserted. A few late shoppers were making their way to the parking lot.

I turned one way, then the other, trying to guess which direction Lucy had headed.

She must have driven here, I decided. Unless she came with Margie and Hannah. When she saw me enter the pizza restaurant, she ducked out to escape to the parking lot.

Walking quickly, I made my way to the exit. I peered into each store I passed, searching the nearly empty aisles for her.

"Whoa!" My heart skipped a beat as I squinted into the Clothes Closet, one of Lucy's favorite stores. I thought I saw her in the back of the store, holding up a pink blouse, discussing it over the counter with a salesgirl.

I turned into the store and began running through the aisle, waving and calling her name. I was halfway to the back when I saw the girl's face clearly.

And realized it wasn't Lucy.

They turned to me, startled. "Can I help you?" the salesgirl asked.

"No, no, thanks," I replied breathlessly. "I—I was looking for someone." I turned and hurried out of the store.

The music cut off as I stepped back into the main

walkway. A strange silence settled over the mall. I heard a baby crying somewhere down the aisle. Shouted voices. The clatter of shopping cart wheels.

Without the background music, they all sounded sort of eerie. Too loud. Not normal.

I stepped out through the first exit I came to. The broad parking lot was nearly deserted. A woman in a bright blue halter top and blue shorts was loading shopping bag after shopping bag into the trunk of a beat-up car. Two little kids were jumping up and down in the backseat.

Several cars were easing out of the lot, turning onto Division Street. Bright headlights rolled over me, forcing me to shield my eyes, as I hurried through row after row, searching for Lucy.

No luck. I was too slow, I realized. She got away.

Angrily, I shoved a shopping cart out of my way. It clattered noisily over the pavement, coming to rest against a curb.

I turned and spotted my car two rows down.

"Hey—!" I cried out in surprise when I saw Lucy—in my body—waiting for me at the side of the car.

chapter

12

"Lucy—hi!" I shouted. "I'm here!"

My sneakers thudded hard over the asphalt as I began running toward her.

"Lucy—you're here! I—I've been searching all over for you!"

Now maybe we can get things straight, I told myself. Maybe Lucy will tell me what's going on.

Even from a distance, she appeared tense. She had both arms down stiffly at her sides, her hands balled into tight fists. "Nicole!" she called.

Not her voice.

Not Lucy's voice.

I stepped up beside her, breathing hard.

"Nicole—we have to talk."

Not her voice. Not her face.

Margie's face.

Margie grabbed me, squeezing my throbbing shoulders with both hands. She turned and called to a car several rows down. "She's here, Hannah. Hannah—I've got Nicole!"

I blinked several times, willing Margie away. Willing Lucy in her place.

But it was Margie. Not Lucy. My eyes had played a cruel trick on me.

"She's right here!" Margie called to Hannah. I saw Hannah step around the other car and start toward us.

"No!" I shrieked.

What were they doing here? Why had they followed me?

"I—I have to find Lucy," I stammered. "I know she told you. I know she told you we switched bodies."

Margie placed a hand on my shoulder. "Calm down, Nicole," she said softly, as if talking to a child. "We just want to talk to you. We just—"

"No!" I screamed. The anger roared through my body. "No!"

They were trying to stop me, trying to hold me there, trying to help Lucy get away.

I shoved Margie out of my way, shoved her with all my strength.

She uttered a surprised yelp and stumbled backward, over the curb. She toppled to the hard surface.

75

Turning, I saw Hannah running toward us. "Wait! Wait!" she called.

But I didn't wait. I pulled open the car door and dived inside. Margie was back on her feet. She reached for the door—as I slammed it.

"Nicole—!" She pounded on the window with both fists. "Nicole—wait! Please!"

I found the key in the ignition. A bad habit of mine. But now I was glad.

I started the car.

Margie pounded on the window. Then she made a grab for the door handle.

I clicked down the door lock.

I shoved the gearshift into Reverse.

Glancing in the rearview mirror, I saw Hannah step up behind the car to block my path.

Wow! I thought. *They really want to stop me from getting to Lucy!*

Hannah waved both hands, signaling for me not to back over her. I stared at her in the rearview mirror. Her cornrow braids blew wildly around her face. Her eyes were wide with fright.

Why were Hannah and Margie so frightened? Why were they so desperate to keep me here?

Had Lucy threatened them?

Had Lucy threatened to murder them, too, if they didn't help her escape?

Margie pounded on my window. Hannah waved wildly from behind the car, blocking my escape.

Uttering a cry of rage, I pulled the gearshift into Drive and slammed my foot down on the gas pedal.

The little Civic let out a roar as it bumped over the curb. My head snapped back as the car jumped onto the narrow square of concrete dividing the rows.

Margie made a last frantic grab for the door handle. Missed. Stumbled back.

I bounced down into the next row. The car shot forward.

I could still hear the two girls shouting my name as I roared away.

I drove around town, trying to calm down, trying to think clearly. But my thoughts circled aimlessly round and around, much like my little car.

So many questions crammed my brain. So many questions that I didn't have answers to.

But Kent can help me.

The words flashed into my troubled mind.

Kent can help me.

The thought swept the questions away. I made a wide U-turn and pressed harder on the gas, heading to Kent's house.

Lucy took all of her clothes, I remembered. That meant she planned to go somewhere. Probably somewhere far away from Shadyside.

She wouldn't leave Shadyside without telling Kent,

I knew. Lucy and Kent were so close. I knew she confided everything to him.

Kent wouldn't talk to me the first time I visited him. But this time, I told myself, I will *make* him talk. I will make him tell me everything. I will force him to tell me where Lucy went.

I thought about my first short meeting with him, hours before. He saw that I looked like Lucy. But he believed me when I said I was really Nicole. And now that I think about it, Kent wasn't shocked at all. That meant he knew that Lucy and I had switched bodies.

That meant he had talked to Lucy this afternoon or evening.

Before Lucy murdered her parents?

Or *after* she had murdered them?

I'll force him to tell me this time, I vowed.

I pulled the car to the curb in front of Kent's house. I gazed over the smooth, sloping lawn to the familiar redbrick house.

Lights were on downstairs. The porchlight was on.

I stepped out of the car and carefully closed the door, careful not to make a sound.

I had decided to surprise Kent, to catch him off guard. To frighten him—just enough to make him tell the truth.

I started up the driveway, keeping in the shadows, away from the square of light that washed onto the lawn from the porch. As I made my way past the front walk and along the side of the house, crickets began to chirp shrilly, as if warning Kent I was coming.

Their whistle grew louder and louder. It sounded deafening to me. I heard every sound, clearer than normal. The scrape of my sneakers on the driveway. The rustle of the wind through the trees along the drive.

As I crept onto the back stoop, the crickets stopped their chirping, as suddenly as they had started. I peered into the window on the kitchen door. A dim light over the stove provided the only brightness.

I turned the knob and pushed. The kitchen door slid open easily.

Leaning on the knob, I pushed the door open all the way, and slipped into the house. The linoleum floor squeaked under my weight.

I stopped. Listened.

I could hear music in the front of the house. Loud rock music from the den.

Good, I thought. It probably means Kent is home alone. He wouldn't be playing the music so loud downstairs if his parents were home.

My eyes darted around the kitchen. They stopped at the knife holder above the white Formica counter.

I crossed the room, studied the knives in the holder, and pulled out a long-bladed kitchen knife.

I'll scare him with this, I told myself.

I'll raise the blade high. I'll back him into a corner. I'll frighten him into talking. I'll make him think that I plan to use it on him—if he doesn't tell me the truth about Lucy. If he doesn't tell me all that he knows.

The knife felt heavy and uncomfortable in my hand. I adjusted my hand around the handle. I always teased Lucy about her tiny hands. I always told her she'd have baby hands for the rest of her life.

Now I wished I had my own hands back. My big, long-fingered hands were stronger. They would have held the kitchen knife more comfortably.

I took a deep breath, edging my way to the front of the house. Thinking hard about how I would play this.

I'll act crazy, I decided. I'll act out of control. I'll raise the knife. I'll scream at him. I'll *make* him tell me where Lucy went.

When Kent has told me what I need to know, I'll apologize, I told myself. I'll ask for his help. I'll confess how eager I am to get my body back.

He'll understand. He'll help me. I know he will.

The music blared louder as I made my way along the front hallway.

I raised the knife and stepped into the den. "Kent? It's me. Nicole. I have to talk—"

I lowered the knife to my side as I stared down at the gruesome sight on the den floor.

Kent's body lay on its back on the tile floor, arms and legs outstretched.

His head had been sliced off.

Puddles of bright red blood had streamed from the neck.

The head stood upright a few feet from the body, propped against the leather couch.

The mouth was frozen open in a wide O of horror. The blue eyes stared lifelessly up at me.

chapter

13

*T*he room started to spin.

I dropped onto the floor. Into a sitting position. I shut my eyes.

When I opened them a few moments later, Kent's blue eyes still stared at me. As I stared in horror, one eyelid slowly drooped, drooped until it closed, leaving Kent's face with a hideous wink.

I swallowed hard, forcing down my nausea.

I shut my eyes. Blinked several times. Hoping, praying that when I looked back, the head would have disappeared. Would have returned to Kent's body.

Sobbing, I raised myself to my knees. "Kent . . ." I murmured his name.

The head had been sliced off. A jagged line across the throat.

The body stretched out calmly over the floor, as if taking a nap. The head stared blankly at its own body.

First the Kramers. And now Kent.

Had Lucy murdered them all?

It made no sense. No sense at all.

Without realizing it, I had climbed to my feet.

I turned away from Kent's headless body. I gazed at the window.

"Oh!" I cried out when I saw the two faces on the other side of the glass. The two grim faces of the gray-suited police officers.

They stared in at me. Stared at the headless corpse on the bloodied den floor. Stared at the kitchen knife still clutched tightly in my hand.

chapter

14

The two faces vanished from the window.

I let the knife fall from my hand. It clattered onto the floor, landing beside Kent's outstretched arm.

They saw me, I realized.

They saw me standing over Kent, holding the knife.

As I backed out of the den, my entire body trembling, I heard the front door click open.

"Don't move!" one of them shouted.

"Nicole. Stay right there."

They knew my name. They knew it was me. Not Lucy.

"But Lucy murdered them all!" I wanted to shout. *"You don't want me! You want Lucy!"*

But I was too terrified to make a sound.

"Don't move." The police officer repeated his instruction.

I turned and bolted to the back door.

I reached the kitchen in time to see the other officer step into the kitchen doorway. "Nicole—don't run away," he said softly. He lowered both hands to his sides. Did he have a gun? Was he about to raise it?

"Nicole—where are you?" His partner's voice from the front.

"No!" I cried, spinning out of the kitchen. Into the narrow back hall. Down the basement stairs two at a time.

I knew this house. I had spent many happy hours at Kent's parties. I knew I could get away. If I was fast enough.

Their shoes clambered heavily down the wooden stairs.

But I was already across the basement. Through the narrow passageway that led to the furnace room.

I heard a crash behind me. Heard one of them utter a shouted curse.

He must have banged his knee or run into something, I figured.

Breathing hard, I plunged into the old coal room. The floor still black and dust-covered from the days when coal was stored here to stoke the furnace.

Up the old coal chute, my sneakers slipping and sliding. I knew the double wooden doors at the top were never locked. With a great heave, I shoved open the doors with both hands.

Cool night air rushed in at me.

I scrabbled out. Scraped my knee on the doorframe. Ignoring the pain that shot up and down my leg, I took a deep breath and gazed around the dark backyard.

Could I make it to my car in front on the street?

Probably not. They'd catch me before I could get inside and start it up.

I turned and began to run.

I was fleeing across the backyard. Climbing over the fence at the back.

Running. Running through dark backyards. Keeping low. Keeping hidden as much as possible.

A trembling, frightened figure fleeing through the darkness.

But where could I go? Where could I hide?

I leaned my back against the wall and struggled to catch my breath.

There was no one following me. I was sure of that. I would have heard them in these silent woods.

I had run all the way to Fear Street. Run blindly, the world a blur, through backyards and alleys, across empty streets, past familiar houses that now seemed strange and unfriendly.

The whole world appeared unfriendly to me now. Worse than that. Threatening.

And so I didn't even hesitate when I reached the Fear Street woods. I ignored the stories I had heard since childhood, the horrifying legends of the street and these woods. Those stories held no fear for me now.

What could be more frightening than my own life?

I plunged into the tangle of trees and shrubs and twining undergrowth. Listening. Listening as I ran for the sounds of my pursuers. The two grim-faced men who wanted to capture me and bring me back—to arrest me for murders only my body committed.

My body. And my friend Lucy.

My best friend.

Somehow I had found the wall. The Changing Wall. The ugly stone structure that had started my troubles.

As it rose up before me in the darkness, I felt my strength ebb away. I knew I couldn't run any farther.

I dropped down, gasping and panting, in front of the wall. I rested against it, closing my eyes, waiting for my breathing to slow, for my pulse to stop pounding.

Waiting . . . and thinking.

About Lucy. My best friend.

Trying to make sense of this.

I pictured her in her room at night, planning this, plotting it. Plotting to kill her mom and dad. And Kent. Figuring out how she could escape her ugly crimes.

Why, Lucy?

I knew she had been having trouble with her parents. I knew she thought they were too strict. I knew the Kramers didn't want her to get so serious about Kent. They liked Kent. They just thought that Lucy and him had become too serious too fast.

And so Lucy had fought and argued with her parents.

But who didn't?

That's what parents and high school students did. It was a normal part of life. Not a happy part of life, but a normal one.

So, why? Why did she choose to murder them both?

And why did she murder Kent? Kent, who cared for her more than anyone in the world. Kent, who had always been so wonderful, so kind and understanding. So much fun.

Kent. Kent.

I kept repeating his name in my mind. Picturing him alive.

I didn't want to picture him as I had seen him tonight in the den. I didn't want to see his out-stretched body, and across the room, his open-mouthed, winking head.

I wanted to see him moving across the room with that sturdy, athletic walk of his, that confident smile, the flashing blue eyes. I wanted to see his blond hair ruffling in the wind as the three of us tossed a Frisbee around during one of our picnics in Shadyside Park.

I wanted to hear his voice. Hear his high, happy laugh.

Never again, I told myself, forcing back the sobs. I pressed the back of my head against the cool stone wall, picturing Kent alive and happy.

Picturing Lucy. In her own body. Not in mine. Not in the body she stole from me to commit her gruesome crimes.

Why, Lucy?

I had always been such a good friend to her. Even when she was mean to me. Even when she acted superior because she had a boyfriend and I didn't. I ignored that side of her. I ignored the part of her that could sometimes be stuck-up and cold.

Because I was her friend. Because I wanted to be there when she needed me.

And when Lucy had the car accident, I was at the hospital every day. I was her only friend who came every day without fail. Her only friend who stuck with her, who never gave up hope.

Even when the doctors had given up, I didn't budge. I knew Lucy would pull through. I never lost hope, never lost my faith in her.

And sure enough, she did pull through.

Lucy was okay, and I was there when we all learned she'd be okay.

I was there. I was always there for you, Lucy.

So where are you now?

Where are you now with my body?

Lost in my troubled thoughts, I struggled to puzzle out what had happened to me on this, the longest day of my life. I shut my eyes. I suddenly felt exhausted.

I hadn't eaten since lunch. My stomach growled, but I didn't feel hungry.

I gazed down at my clothes. Lucy's clothes. The tights torn and stained. The short skirt twisted.

My hand went to the pack around my waist. My wallet. I had my wallet in the pack.

Shaking my head, I pulled it out. Was it my wallet or Lucy's?

I held it up and examined it in the narrow shaft of moonlight that filtered down between the trees.

My wallet.

I unzipped it. I don't know why. What did I hope to find?

I slapped at a mosquito on my arm. The wallet dropped to the ground. As I reached down for it, I had an idea.

A desperate idea. A crazy idea.

But if it worked . . .

I dug feverishly into the wallet. It was so hard to see. And my fingers were trembling with excitement.

A few seconds later I found it and plucked it out. An old class photo of Lucy.

I tucked everything back into my wallet, zipped it, and shoved the wallet back into the pack. Then I raised the little photo close to examine it in the dim light.

It was a funny photo. Lucy always hated it.

She had her blond hair pulled straight back. But a thick strand had come loose and stood out at the side of her forehead.

The photographer's light reflected in Lucy's eyes, making them appear to sparkle. But her smile was crooked. And she had a tiny smudge on her chin which looked like a pimple.

Lucy hated the photo so much, she wouldn't give them out to her friends. But she gave me one—on the condition that I put it away and never showed it to anyone.

And now, examining the photo, I climbed to my feet. I ignored my aching muscles and hauled myself onto the wall.

"Whoa!" I struggled to keep my balance. The top of the wall was so narrow and uneven.

This has to work! I told myself.

My crazy scheme. My frantic idea.

To hold Lucy's photo in one hand. And jump to the other side of the wall.

Maybe—just maybe—the magic will work for a photograph. And our bodies will switch back. And I will be Nicole again.

Maybe . . . maybe . . .

Please work! I prayed.

I grasped the photo of Lucy tightly in my right hand. Held the hand out to my side as if I were holding hands once again with Lucy.

And then I jumped off the wall.

chapter

15

I landed on both feet on the soft dirt.

I knew immediately that it hadn't worked.

Lucy's photo was still gripped in my hand. Lucy's hand. Lucy's pudgy little hand.

That was all I needed to see to know that my plan had failed. But I examined myself anyway, desperately hoping that somehow I had changed back to me.

But no. I was still wearing Lucy's black hightop sneakers, her tights, now dirt-stained and torn, her short skirt. I grabbed at my hair. Lucy's hair, shorter and finer-textured than mine.

Lucy. Lucy. Lucy.

I needed the real Lucy here with me in order to get my body back.

But how could I find her? Where had she escaped to?

I yawned wearily. I suddenly realized how exhausted I felt. Every muscle in my body ached. My head throbbed. It took such an effort to hold my eyes open.

Yawning again, I lowered myself to the damp ground. I settled back against the wall and shut my eyes. The cold stones pressed against my back and head.

With a sigh I curled up in the dirt. And fell into a deep, dreamless sleep.

I lifted my head, squinting against the morning sunlight. A scrawny, brown rabbit peered suspiciously at me across the dirt. Its nose twitched and its pointed ears arched straight up.

With a groan I pulled myself to a sitting position. The rabbit whipped around, silently vanishing into the tall grass.

It took me a few seconds to remember where I was.

I brushed dirt and a wet leaf off my arm. My back ached from sleeping on the hard ground. My throat felt dry. I wanted to brush my teeth, brush the sour taste from my mouth.

As I stood up, a dozen thoughts jumbled into my head at once. Sleep had cleared my mind. But now the frightening questions rushed back in.

Mom and Dad must be frantic, I thought. They must be desperate to know where I am.

But then I remembered that I was Lucy, not Nicole.

Did Lucy go home to my house? If she did, my parents probably weren't worried at all. They would go off to work this morning, thinking their daughter Nicole was safe and sound.

I brushed the hair back off my face. A large black beetle had crawled into my hair during the night. It dropped onto my hand. I tossed it to the ground.

I'm a disgusting mess, I realized. I need a shower. I need fresh clothes.

I glanced at my watch. A little after seven.

My parents left for work promptly at seven-thirty. It would be easy to sneak into the house, get myself cleaned up, and change into clean clothes.

My clothes would be a little big on Lucy's body. But she and I had traded things before.

I stretched, trying to force away the aches, trying to get my muscles working. Then I made my way through the woods to the street.

It was a hazy, hot morning. The air felt heavy and still. The morning dew stained my sneakers as I trudged through the grass and weeds.

I kept away from the street, keeping low as I walked through front yards and alleys. A rolled-up morning newspaper in a driveway made me stop.

I glanced up at the house. No one seemed to be stirring inside. I picked up the newspaper and began to unroll it.

Would Lucy's murders be on the front page?

Would the story tell about how the police are on my trail?

My eyes swept rapidly over the newspaper.

No story. No story on the front page.

I pulled the paper open. Two colorful ad sheets fell onto the driveway. I searched the next pages. And the next.

Confused, I folded the paper up and set it back on the driveway. I glanced again at the house. No one watching from the windows.

I hurried on, thinking hard.

Why weren't the three murders reported in the paper?

Were the police keeping the story quiet until they had captured me?

Was it possible that no one had discovered the Kramers' bodies yet?

That was possible, I realized. But the two policemen had seen Kent's body. And they had seen me standing over Kent with the kitchen knife in my hand.

So why wasn't his murder reported in the paper?

The police are keeping it quiet for a reason, I decided. They're waiting till they capture me. Then they'll release the whole story at once.

The story seemed to make sense. As much sense as everything else that had happened to me since yesterday.

I saw my parents' car backing down the driveway as I turned the corner. I ducked behind the wide trunk of an old maple tree and watched them drive away.

My dad wasn't wearing his usual blue suit. He looked a mess. Mom looked worried. I didn't know what to do. I couldn't deal with this now.

I had the strong urge to call to them, to go running after them. To cry: "It's me, Mom and Dad! It's really me! I know I don't look like me. But it's me!"

I wanted to hug them and hold them both close. And tell them what had happened. Tell them the horrors I had seen. Tell them about the murders Lucy had committed in my body.

But I knew they wouldn't believe me.

My parents are practical, common-sense-type people. They're very smart, but they don't have great imaginations.

No way they'd believe I was their daughter Nicole.

Seeing them drive away made me feel even more desperate and afraid. I sneaked into the house through the kitchen door. I was surprised they left it unlocked. Then I made my way upstairs.

I took a long shower and shampooed my hair three times. I wanted to stay under the hot water forever, so warm and cleansing.

I nearly burst into tears when I entered my room. It looked so pretty and neat. The bed was made. The clutter on my desk had been straightened.

This is my home, I thought with a sob. This is where I belong.

But will I ever be able to live in my own house again?

I changed into a pair of faded denim jeans and a

white T-shirt. I brushed my hair—Lucy's hair—back and fastened it in a ponytail.

I spent a long time staring at Lucy's face in my dressing table mirror.

Why had I ever agreed to switch bodies with her? Was I *that* unhappy? That desperately unhappy?

As I stared into the mirror, two other faces floated into my mind. Margie and Hannah.

Margie and Hannah knew where Lucy had gone.

They had to know. They were so eager to keep me from going after Lucy, so eager to keep me from finding her.

Lucy must have told them everything.

I stood up and stepped away the mirror.

"I'll go to school," I said out loud. "I'll find Margie or Hannah. I'll make them tell."

I glanced at the clock on my nightstand. A little after eight. Homeroom starts at eight-twenty. Plenty of time to get to school and find one of them.

I didn't want to leave the house. I didn't want to leave my room.

But I knew I had no choice.

I took all the money I kept in my top dresser drawer—about forty dollars in fives and singles—and jammed it into my jeans pockets. In the kitchen I grabbed a cherry Pop Tart from the box and ate it cold. I slugged down some orange juice from the carton. Took another Pop-Tart for the road.

Then I made my way out of the house, being careful to close the kitchen door securely behind me.

Margie and Hannah. Hannah and Margie.

Their faces hovered in front of me as I hurried to school. Margie was in my homeroom. I wasn't sure about Hannah. I thought she was somewhere on the second floor near the music room.

Walking quickly, my heart pounding excitedly, I turned the corner onto Park Drive. The front of the redbrick high school came into view.

Most kids were already inside. But a few latecomers were hurrying to the front doors.

I started to jog up the long walk to the entrance. Halfway there I stopped when I saw the two gray figures on either side of the doors.

The two gray-suited police officers.

Watching everyone.

Waiting for me.

Did they see me?

chapter

16

I turned sharply. Began walking toward the street. Not running. But taking long, rapid strides.

The North Shadyside bus pulled up to the stop in front of the high school. I hurried to the bus, planning to jump on.

But the bus was filled with kids arriving for school. They piled off one by one, blocking my escape.

Were the two officers chasing after me? I didn't dare glance back.

Hurry, hurry! I silently urged the kids jumping down from the bus. Luckily, none of my friends was onboard.

Finally I climbed into the bus. The doors closed

behind me. The driver turned the wheel, and the bus pulled away from the curb.

I turned, lowered my head, trying to see out the glass door. The two officers remained at their posts at the school entrance. They hadn't spotted me.

I turned to see the driver, an old man with a red face and bright blue eyes, squinting at me suspiciously. "Shouldn't you be in school?" he asked, slowing at a stop sign.

"I—I'm sick," I lied. "I—" I realized I didn't have any change. Just the money I had jammed into my jeans pocket.

"Pull over!" I cried. "Please!"

The driver frowned, but obediently pulled the bus to the curb.

"I—I'd better get out," I stammered.

He opened the door. I leaped down to the street. "Sorry!" I called back to him. But he had already closed the door behind me.

I watched the bus roar away. Then I gazed around. I had traveled exactly one block. Just far enough to escape the eyes of the two policemen.

But now what?

I still needed to talk to Margie or Hannah.

I can't spend the rest of my life running from those two cops, I told myself unhappily. I have to find Lucy. Fast!

I crept back toward the school, thinking hard. I wondered if there were officers at the back, too.

Keeping behind a tall hedge, I made my way toward the back of the school.

"Hey—what are you doing there?"

I let out a startled cry. Turning, I saw a woman holding a garden hose in the middle of the yard. "What are you doing in my yard?"

"Sorry," I called to her. "I'm just going to school."

"This isn't a shortcut!" she called sharply.

I hurried through a break in the hedge out to the sidewalk.

The back of the school was guarded, too, I saw. Two other officers had been posted at the door across from the student parking lot.

I ran across the street and pressed up close to the tall fence that ran along the football stadium. I stopped there to catch my breath.

I could hear the first bell ring. The kids were all inside now, except for a boy frantically pedaling his bike toward the bike rack.

Keeping in the shadow of the fence, I took a few steps closer to the back of the school. I had a good view of the two officers. They were shaking their heads, frowning as they talked.

Giving up.

They thought I'd show up for school and they'd grab me, I decided. But now they're giving up in disappointment.

I was right. I watched them step away from the back doors. They disappeared around toward the front, probably joining the other two officers.

I waited a few seconds, making sure they weren't returning. Then I made a wild dash to the building.

I had a plan. A plan to see Margie.

I pulled open the back door and ducked inside. It took a few seconds for my eyes to adjust to the dim light of the corridor. The hall was empty. Everyone had gone into their homerooms.

The second bell rang as I crept to the gym, just around the corner to the right. I pushed open the door and hurried inside.

No one there. The gym already felt like an oven, first thing in the morning. Glancing up at the bleachers, I saw that one end of a GO, TIGERS banner had come loose. The banner tilted over the top seats.

My sneakers squeaked over the polished floor as I trotted to the girls' locker room. Margie had gym fourth period. Same as me.

My plan was to hide in the locker room until then.

Then I would pull Margie aside and confront her, force her to tell me where Lucy was.

I pulled open the locker room door and stepped inside. The room felt cooler than the gym. I heard the *plink plink* of water dripping in the shower room.

Where to hide?

I hurried past the rows of wooden benches and dark lockers. Someone had left a black hightop sneaker on the floor, and I stumbled over it.

At the back wall stood a small equipment closet. The door was half open. I pulled it open all the way and peered inside.

Empty. Glancing down, I thought I saw a dead mouse curled up on the closet floor. But as I squinted at it, I realized it was a clump of dust.

I heard voices. Behind me at the locker room door. Moving quickly, I slipped into the empty closet and pulled the door almost closed.

I backed into the darkness until I pressed up against the closet wall. The air smelled stale and sour. I'd left the door open a crack. Now I heard more voices, girls' voices that I recognized, the shuffle of feet, the clatter of gym lockers being opened. They were getting changed for first-period gym.

This is going to be a long wait, I told myself with a silent sigh. But it will be worth it if I can find Margie and force her to tell me about Lucy.

I carefully lowered myself to a sitting position on the closet floor. My hand fell over the clump of dust. I brushed it away.

I knew that no one would open the closet door and discover me. There was no reason for anyone to go into this closet.

Locker doors slammed. The room became quieter as girls headed out to the gym. I could hear the thump of basketballs. I heard Miss Hawkins' whistle blow.

Leaning back against the closet wall, I shut my eyes and let myself be swallowed up by the darkness. It was already starting to get hot and sticky inside the closet. But I didn't dare step out. There were always girls coming in and out of the locker room once the day started.

I can make it till fourth period, I assured myself.

I decided the wait would give me some quiet time to think. To think about Lucy and why she murdered the three people she cared about most. To try to figure out why she hated me so much, why she left me to take the blame.

The hours passed. Girls changed and played basketball, then changed again to go to their next class.

But I didn't think of any answers. It was as if the answers hovered just beyond my reach, just beyond a thick wall of fog. And no matter how I struggled, I couldn't clear away the fog.

When the fourth-period bell finally rang, I shook away my confused thoughts and climbed to my feet. Alert to every sound, I listened to the girls' voices as they piled into the locker room, voices I knew so well.

I could hear Margie kidding around with two other girls. So near. She was so near, I knew I could push open the closet door, reach out, and grab her.

But I waited. Margie was always one of the last to change, always one of the last to leave the locker room. I hoped she would linger behind today. I hoped I could confront her without a dozen other girls in the way.

I pressed both hands against the door, preparing to spring out. I listened hard. I had to catch her before she ran out to the gym.

My heart started to pound. The voices all blended together in my ears. I tried to shut them all out, all except Margie's.

A shrill cry made my heart jump.

I heard other frightened cries. Shuffling noises. Loud shouts. The thud of running feet.

What has happened? I wondered.

What is all the commotion?

I pushed open the closet door and plunged out into the locker room.

I saw a cluster of girls in their gym shorts and T-shirts. Their faces were tight with fear.

They were gaping down at a girl on the floor. A girl sprawled on her back on the locker room floor.

"Margie?" I cried.

Yes. It was Margie.

chapter

17

I pushed into the circle of girls. No one seemed to notice me. They all stared down at Margie.

Margie raised herself high enough to grab her left calf. Her face twisted in pain. "Oh, wow!" she cried. "These leg cramps are the *worst!*"

"You just don't want to play today," another girl joked. "You don't want to get sweaty because it's class photo day."

Everyone laughed. Tense laughter.

"You really scared me when you screamed like that," someone told Margie.

"I frightened *myself,*" Margie groaned, rubbing the calf. "It's starting to feel a little better."

I took a step back, then another.

No one had noticed me yet. They all leaned over Margie. Two girls helped her to her feet. Margie hobbled to a low wooden bench and sat down.

I slipped back behind the closet door.

I heard Miss Hawkins's whistle blow out in the gym.

"Go ahead," Margie told the others. "I'm okay. I'll be out in a second."

This is a lucky break for me, I thought. About time I had a lucky break.

I waited for the others to leave. Then I stepped out quickly. "Hi, Margie."

Bent over, rubbing her leg, she sat up with a start. "Nicole—!" Her face filled with surprise. "You're here?"

I moved in front of her, ready to stop her if she tried to run. I pressed my hands against my waist. "Where's Lucy?" I demanded. My voice came out in a choked whisper.

"Huh?" Margie pretended she didn't hear me.

"I need to find Lucy," I said through gritted teeth. "I'm not kidding around, Margie. You know where Lucy is, and I need to find out. I have to get her to switch bodies back."

Margie raised herself to her feet. She winced in pain. I guessed her leg muscle was still cramped.

"Nicole—sit down," she said softly. She pointed to the bench. I couldn't read her expression. Was it fear? Was she thinking frantically? Trying to think of how to stall me, how to keep me from finding Lucy?

"I don't want to sit down," I said coldly. "I want to

find Lucy. Right away. I want to get out of her body, Margie. And you're going to help me."

Margie bit her lower lip. Her dark eyes locked on to mine. I could see her studying me, trying to decide just how serious I was.

I needed her help so badly. I felt so desperate, so angry and frightened and desperate, all at the same time. Suddenly the words just came bursting out of me.

"Margie, she took me into the woods," I said, squeezing Margie's bare arm. "She took me to the Changing Wall. We switched bodies. She told you all this—right? She told you?"

Margie didn't reply. She continued to stare at me. I could see she was thinking hard.

"But she didn't tell you about the murders," I continued, holding on to her arm. "She didn't tell you she killed her parents and she killed Kent. That's why I have to get my body back. Do you understand? Do you understand why you have to help me?"

I saw her swallow hard. She gently removed her arm from my grasp. "Changing Wall?" she murmured.

"I'll take you there," I told her. "I'll show you. I'll show you where we switched. But then—"

Her eyes narrowed. "Nicole, if I go with you, will you make me a promise?" she asked, speaking softly and slowly, as if talking to a child.

"Promise?" I demanded suspiciously. I didn't trust her. She had already helped Lucy escape once. "What kind of promise?"

She rubbed the back of her calf. "If I go with you to the Changing Wall, will you come back here with me? Will you come back with me and sit tight until I get your parents?"

"No!" I answered quickly. "I can't see my parents until I have my body back. I have to know where Lucy is! You can't keep it from me any longer!"

Her mouth dropped open. But she didn't reply.

"Do you know where Lucy is?" I screamed, losing control. "Do you?"

"Y-yes," she admitted. "But, Nicole—"

The locker room door swung open. I heard voices. Footsteps.

Uttering a low cry, I slipped back into the closet. I tried to pull the door closed only partway. But I pulled too hard and the door clicked shut.

The voices on the other side were muffled. I couldn't make out the words. I figured someone had come in to check on Margie and see if she was okay.

What bad timing, I thought bitterly, trying to calm my pounding heart. Margie had just confessed that she knew where Lucy was. She was about to tell me where I could find her.

I pressed against the door, listening hard.

Was Margie telling the intruder about me? Was she telling the other girl to go get Miss Hawkins? Was she planning to trap me in this closet, to keep me here and go get my parents?

No. Please! I silently begged. *Please, Margie. Please don't betray me like Lucy did.*

109

I pressed harder against the door, trying to hear what they were saying.

But the room was silent now.

Had the other girl left?

I clicked the closet door, pushed it open slowly, and peeked around it.

"No!"

I uttered a hoarse cry as I saw Margie. On her back on the floor again.

chapter
18

Not a leg cramp this time.

I saw the puddle of blood widening around her.

Saw that her head had been crushed in. Her skull cracked. Her cheek bashed in. One eye smashed shut.

Saw the shot put on the floor beside her. The blood-smeared shot put.

And I knew that Lucy had struck again.

Lucy had crept into the locker room and murdered Margie. Crushed her head with a shot put.

Crushed her. Crushed her and walked back out.

My entire body convulsed in a violent shudder. I forced myself to turn away from the gruesome sight.

Lucy, how could you?

The question burned into my mind.

How could you kill so coldly?

Miss Hawkins's shrill whistle on the other side of the locker room door snapped me from my horrifying thoughts. I raised my eyes to the door.

Someone is going to come in here, I realized. Someone is going to see me. Someone is going to find me standing here over Margie's battered body.

I spun around, fighting back my panic.

The locker room had two doors. One led to the gym. The other led out to the hall.

I had no choice. I turned and hurried out into the hall.

I stopped just outside the door and glanced both ways.

No one there.

I took a deep breath and started to run. I had to get out of the building without being seen.

I ran full speed. I practically flew.

I prayed that no one would come around the corner and recognize me.

Please, please—let me get away!

A few seconds later I hurtled through the back doors and ran across the student parking lot. I didn't stop running until I was two blocks from the school.

Then I collapsed on the tall grass in an empty lot, my sides aching, my temples throbbing. I sat with my mouth open, panting like a dog, sweat running down my cheeks.

Lucy is following me.

She's following me everywhere I go.

The thought broke into my mind. I felt a cold shiver run down my back.

Why hadn't I realized it before?

I visited Kent. And then she killed Kent.

I came to see Margie. And then she killed Margie.

Without realizing it, I jumped to my feet. I cupped my hands around my mouth and shouted, "Lucy— are you here?" My voice came out hoarse and breathless.

I received no answer.

"Lucy—can you see me? Are you watching me?" I screamed. "I know you're here! Where are you, Lucy?"

No answer.

I dropped back onto the grass.

My head was spinning. I felt so frightened and so completely alone.

I had no idea what to do next.

I wandered around most of the day. I didn't even remember where I had been or what I had been thinking.

Did I eat any lunch or dinner? I didn't remember.

At dark I found myself back at the gray stone wall in the Fear Street woods. I don't know why I kept returning there. Maybe I figured Lucy might show up.

Of course that didn't happen.

I pressed against the wall and drifted into another deep, dreamless sleep.

At dawn I awoke with a face in my mind. A round,

pleasant face, a pale face surrounded by short curls of salt-and-pepper hair.

The face of Lucy's grandmother.

I sat up and stretched. My whole body ached from sleeping on the hard ground. My clothes felt damp from the morning dew.

Slowly I climbed to my feet and brushed myself off. A huge red ball of a sun still hung low over the trees. The air carried a morning coolness.

The smiling face of Lucy's grandmother lingered in my mind.

When Lucy wasn't getting along with her parents— which was a lot of the time—she always went to visit Grandma Carla. Lucy and her grandmother were very close.

Is Lucy finished following me around? I wondered. Now that she has murdered four people in my body, has she decided to make her escape?

I remembered that she had taken all of the clothes from her bedroom closet. That meant she planned to go away somewhere.

And Grandma Carla's farm seemed the most logical place she would go.

Of course, if Lucy went there, Grandma Carla would see my body and think that it was me. But she wouldn't find it unusual for me to visit.

Several years, Lucy and I had spent parts of our summer vacations up there. Grandma Carla was like a grandmother to me, too.

As I made my way out of the woods, I struggled to

remember the small farm town where Grandma Carla had her farm.

Conklin. The name popped into my mind. Yes. Conklin.

I reached into my jeans pocket and pulled out the wad of bills I had grabbed from home. All of my savings.

I counted it as I walked. Yes. More than enough money to get some breakfast. And then buy a bus ticket to Conklin.

I turned the corner onto Mill Road. I saw Alma's, the little coffee shop, across the street. I'll use the rest room to get cleaned up, I decided. I'll buy some breakfast. And I'll hurry to the bus station.

Crossing the street, I suddenly felt a little more hopeful.

I had a strong hunch. A real premonition.

Somehow I knew that I was about to find Lucy at last.

The bus to Conklin didn't leave until two in the afternoon. Then the driver had to stop to fix a flat tire a few miles north of Waynesbridge.

As we bumped over the narrow highway that led through the small farm towns, I began to feel more and more nervous.

What shall I say to Grandma Carla? I wondered.

Of course, I'll have to pretend to be Lucy. She wouldn't understand about our switching bodies. And she's so frail, I don't want to give her a shock.

So I'll pretend to be Lucy. And I'll ask if Nicole is visiting.

And then what? I asked myself.

What will Lucy do when she sees I've caught up to her? Will she run again? Will she try to kill me, too?

My best friend . . .

Staring out at the endless green fields, I kept thinking how Lucy was my best friend. Best friend. Best friend.

I repeated the words in my mind until they had no meaning.

Grandma Carla's farm stood a little less than a quarter mile from the Conklin bus stop. I watched the bus rumble away and began to walk along the soft, grassy shoulder of the narrow highway.

Wildflowers bloomed in the field to my left. The tall grasses swayed in a soft breeze.

A column of silvery gnats rose up in front of me. The gnats—thousands of them—circled wildly, silently, like a soft, silver cyclone.

I stepped onto the road to walk around them. A few seconds later Grandma Carla's barn came into view. It had been painted white at one time. I remembered it sparkling in the sunlight as Lucy and I ran inside to explore and climb the hay bales. But now the paint was cracked and peeling, the dark boards showing through.

Behind the barn stood the old farmhouse. A two-story white structure, the house had seemed enormous when Lucy and I were kids. But now it looked like a small, old-fashioned house with its open back porch and shuttered windows.

"Lucy, are you in there?" I murmured as I eased myself over the rail fence and started across the tall grass of the backyard to the house.

"Lucy, I'm coming. I know I'm going to find you now."

I stepped up onto the back porch, the old boards creaking under my sneakers. I made my way to the kitchen. And knocked loudly on the door.

part three

The Reunion

chapter

19

"Oh, goodness! Hello!" Grandma Carla let out a squeal of surprise. A smile wrinkled her round face. She pushed open the screen door for me.

"How *are* you?" I cried, wrapping her in a hug.

Her tiny body felt frail, almost brittle. I loosened my hug and stepped back to look at her.

Her gray-blue eyes were as bright as ever. But the rest of her face had faded. She was tinier and more birdlike than I recalled. She reminded me of the flamingos I'd seen one summer in Florida. Like a flamingo whose pink color had faded to powder white.

"It's so good to see you," she said, grinning at me. "I—I'm just so shocked." She placed a hand over the chest of her pale blue housedress.

She led the way toward the kitchen table against the wall. She walked slowly, a small step at a time. I guessed that her arthritis was bothering her.

The house smelled of roast chicken. I saw a large soup pot steaming on the stove. I suddenly remembered I hadn't eaten since breakfast.

I turned to see Grandma Carla leaning both hands on a chairback, staring hard at me. She scratched her curly hair. "Now, let me see . . . When were you here last? Two summers ago? Yes. I believe it was."

"I think so, Grandma," I said uncertainly. I gazed around her toward the front of the house. "Is Nicole here?" I blurted out.

"What?" She narrowed her eyes at me.

"Is Nicole here?" I repeated. "Nicole told me she might be coming up here to visit you. So I thought . . ."

I couldn't read Grandma Carla's expression at all. Her bottom lip quivered. And she stared thoughtfully at me.

Did Lucy show up here in my body? I wondered, staring back at the old woman.

Did Lucy warn her not to tell that she was here?

"Come sit down," Grandma Carla said, pulling out the kitchen chair for me. "When did you leave Shadyside? This morning?"

"A little after two," I told her.

She raised her eyes to the sunburst clock above the double sink. "It's nearly five-thirty. You must be starving."

"I—I am kind of hungry," I replied.

"Sit down," she urged. "It's lucky I put up a pot of soup. I don't usually make so much since it's just me. But today . . ."

You made a big pot because Lucy is here, I thought to myself.

"Please. Sit down," she insisted.

I obediently walked over to the table and sat down in the wooden high-backed chair. I turned when I heard her shuffle from the room. "Grandma Carla, you didn't answer my question," I called after her. "Is Nicole here?"

"Back in a minute," she called. "We'll have a nice talk."

Something about the way she said that made me suspicious. I felt a knot of dread form in my stomach.

Quietly I climbed up from the chair. I crept into the hallway, following her, keeping my back pressed against the wall.

I was a few feet from the living room when I heard her on the phone.

Calling the police.

chapter

20

I turned to the kitchen. My first thought was to run. To get out of there, away from the farm.

But I stopped and stood frozen in the hallway.

I had come so far. And I had been running for so long.

I can't keep running, I told myself.

I have to get my body back. I have to get my life back.

I burst into the living room just as Grandma Carla hung up the phone. She turned, startled. "Oh—!"

I stormed up to her angrily, my hands balled into tight fists. "Why?" I demanded in a trembling voice.

She stared back but didn't answer. I could see fear growing in her eyes.

"Why?" I repeated. My body began to shake with rage. I felt myself going out of control.

"It will be okay. I called for help," she said. She tried to back away from me, but I followed her. She suddenly looked even more frail and birdlike.

"I—I trusted you!" I cried. "I've always trusted you. Why did you call them? Why won't you *help* me?"

Her blue eyes stared hard into mine. "Let's sit down and talk about it, okay?" she suggested softly.

Sit and wait for the police to come and grab me? And haul me away for murders I didn't commit?

Her quiet suggestion made me even angrier. "I just came to find Nicole," I told the old woman through gritted teeth. "Nicole is here—isn't she! Isn't she!"

Grandma Carla didn't reply. She bit her lower lip. Her lips had lost all color, had become as pale as her face.

Her eyes went to the living room window. I knew she was watching for the police car.

I reached out and grabbed both of her arms. "Just tell me where Nicole is," I pleaded. "Please—tell me where she is, and I'll go. I promise I'll leave and never come back."

I must have squeezed her arms too hard. Grandma Carla winced in pain. I loosened my grip, but I held on to her.

I had the feeling that if I let go, she would slip away. Vanish into thin air. Leave me alone to face the police.

"I don't know where she is," Grandma Carla replied, her eyes on the big picture window.

"Why won't you tell me the truth?" I screamed.

I thought I heard a car crunching over gravel. I dropped her frail, bonelike arms. I spun away.

I had no choice, I realized. I had to run. Lucy's grandmother wasn't going to help me—even though she thought I was Lucy.

"Wait! Come back!" she called as I ran to the back. "Please wait!"

I ignored her shouts, shoved open the kitchen door, and plunged out into the backyard. A soft breeze rustled the cornstalks in the field behind the barn.

I turned one way, then the other, searching for a hiding place. I knew I couldn't run far. I was too weary. Too tired of running.

My eyes stopped at the old stone well to the right of the barn. The water was contaminated. The well hadn't been used in years.

Could I hide inside it? Hang on to the stones on the side? Wedge myself in?

No, I decided. Too scary.

What if I fell? Plunged down into the filthy water? I'd drown before anyone could find me and drag me out.

Could I hide in the cornfield?

Maybe for a while. But the corn wasn't quite as tall as me. I'd have to stoop and crawl. The police would find me easily. An open field couldn't hide me for long.

I heard a car door slam. Beside the house.

The sound forced me to move.

I began running across the tall grass to the barn. I had no choice, I decided. They'd search the barn. But there were good hiding places inside. I could bury myself in a mound of hay or straw. Or squeeze into the old tool closet behind the tractor stall.

I heard a second car door slam. The sound sent a jolt down my body, tightening my leg muscles, making my heart pound.

Running as hard as I could, I bolted into the barn. My feet slid on the straw that blanketed the dirt floor. I stopped for a moment, allowing my eyes to adjust to the darkness.

The air felt cool. I gasped in a deep breath. Another. It smelled so sweet.

So many memories came flooding back to me, triggered by the familiar aromas of the barn. So many wonderful days, so many happy moments.

I forced back a sob.

I knew I had no time for memories. Gray light filtered down from the dirty window in the hayloft above me. In the dim light I saw a tall pile of straw against the side wall, neatly stacked in tied bundles.

I could hide behind it, I told myself.

But isn't that the first place they will search?

I took a few steps deeper into the barn. I stopped when I heard a rustling sound. The scrape of dry straw.

Footsteps?

No. Probably a field mouse, I told myself.

My eyes searched for a hiding place. I saw Grandma Carla's rusted old tractor in the corner stall. I could duck behind it, I told myself, scrunch down behind the back tires.

But they'd find me there easily.

The straw pile was the best place, I told myself. For now, anyway. It would hide me for a while. And I could peer out from behind it and watch the police trying to find me.

The dry straw on the barn floor crackled beneath my sneakers as I made my way to the tall bundles. I slipped behind the tallest bundle.

And bumped into another person hiding back there.

"Oh!" I let out a startled shriek.

And then I recognized her.

"Lucy!" I cried. "You *are* here!"

chapter

21

She gaped at me in shock.

We grabbed on to each other.

I had been so angry, so furious at her. But now, to my surprise, I felt glad to see her.

The chase is over, I thought. No more running.

In the gray light from the loft window above, I stared at her. Stared at my face. My body.

She wore a dark blue, long-sleeved top of mine over white tennis shorts. Her brown hair fell loosely over her shoulders.

I wrapped my arms around her waist and hugged her.

I let go when she didn't respond, didn't hug me back.

"You're here," I repeated. "I finally found you."

She narrowed her eyes—my eyes—at me.

She still hadn't said a word.

I felt overcome by emotion. A dozen emotions all at once.

I felt angry and relieved and joyful and confused all at once.

"Lucy—why?" I managed to choke out. "Why did you do it? Why did you . . . kill them? And why did you run from me?"

She lowered her eyes. "I can't explain," she whispered.

"You *have* to explain!" I cried. I leaned past the straw to check the barn door. No sign of the police officers. Yet.

"You *have* to explain, Lucy!" I repeated in a trembling voice. "And we have to switch back."

She mumbled a reply. I couldn't hear it. She continued to avoid my stare.

"I want my body back," I insisted. "I want to switch back our bodies—now! Do you hear me?"

She finally raised her eyes to me, sad eyes, cold eyes. "We can't switch back," she said softly.

"Huh? Why not?" I demanded angrily.

"I'm not Lucy," she replied. "Lucy switched bodies with me this afternoon. My name is Nancy."

chapter

22

"You're lying," I told her, feeling my anger grow. "You're lying, Lucy."

She shook her head. Her dark eyes brimmed with tears.

"I don't believe you," I insisted. "You can cry all you want to. I'm not stupid. Do you really think I'm stupid enough to believe you?"

Her chin trembled. The large tears rolled slowly down her cheeks. She made no effort to wipe them away.

"It's the truth," she whispered. "I don't care if you believe me or not. I don't even know your name."

"My name is Nicole," I replied through clenched

teeth. "But I'm inside Lucy's body. And you're in mine—*Lucy!*"

I repeated her name again and again, so angry, so out of control, so desperate for her to be Lucy and not some stranger.

"Lucy, Lucy, Lucy!"

"Stop it!" she pleaded. "Stop!" She held her hands over her ears and shut her eyes.

"Lucy, Lucy, Lucy!"

I wanted to grab her and shake her, shake her hard. Shake her till she confessed that she really was Lucy.

"I'm not Lucy!" she insisted. "I'm Nancy. Lucy *forced* me to switch. She *forced* me. Then she—she took my body and she ran away."

More tears rolled down her face. Her whole body began to tremble.

I took a step back, watching her. I realized I was beginning to believe her. "You—you really aren't Lucy?" I stammered.

She shook her head. Tears fell onto the straw on the barn floor. "She forced me to switch. *Now* what am I going to do?"

I heard the scrape of straw. Heavy thuds. I turned to see a dark figure enter the barn.

The police.

"We've got to hide," I whispered.

To my surprise, Nancy had a smile on her face. Her dark eyes gleamed.

"The police are here," I warned, whispering softly. "We have to hide."

Her grin widened. She shook her head. "Nicole, you really are an idiot!" she said. "You really believed that dumb story!"

"Lucy!" I cried.

She nodded, grinning triumphantly.

She had fooled me. There was no Nancy. She was Lucy. I had found her.

I made an angry grab for her. But she sidestepped away. Then she spun around the bundle of straw and started to run.

"Hey—!" I called in a whisper.

I forgot about the police. I started to chase after her. I couldn't let her get away again.

In the dimming gray light I saw her dart out through the barn door. I ran harder. I was only ten or twenty steps behind her.

She ran toward the old well, her sneakers pounding the ground, her brown hair flying wildly behind her.

Crickets chirped shrilly all around. I heard a dog howling mournfully in the distance.

It was as if the entire farm had suddenly come alive. As if all the plants and creatures around me were sounding their excitement.

I squinted in the darkness, my eyes locked on Lucy. She was running hard, only a few yards from the old well now.

What did she plan to do? I wondered. Did she plan to hide in there?

I tried to run faster, to catch up with her.

But I heard the thud of footsteps behind me.

I heard a groan. Heavy breathing. And then I felt strong arms wrap around my legs.

"Ohhhh!" I uttered a startled cry as I was tackled and dragged to the ground.

"Let me go!" I shrieked. "I can't let her get away again!"

But the two hands held me down.

I kicked my legs, thrashed my arms frantically. I couldn't get away.

With an angry cry I turned to face my pursuer.

When I gazed into his face, I gasped in horror.

"Kent!" I choked out. "Kent—no! It can't be you! You're dead! You're dead!"

He narrowed his eyes at me coldly. "Nicole, I've come for you," he said.

chapter

23

*H*e let go of me and climbed to his feet. Then he reached out for my hands and pulled me up.

His hands were warm. He was breathing hard.

"Kent—you're dead," I murmured. "I saw you. Your head—" The words choked in my throat.

"I'm okay," he replied softly.

"No," I insisted. "I was in your house. I saw you in your den. I saw the blood, Kent. I was there."

He placed a calming hand on my trembling shoulder. "Ssshhhh," he whispered. "Take a deep breath, Nicole. Try to calm down. I followed you here. I've come to help you."

I obeyed his instruction. But I knew it would take more than a deep breath to calm me down.

I felt too confused, too frightened. I had too many questions.

How did he find me?

Why did he come?

Who did I see lying dead on the floor in Kent's den?

"Kent—" I started.

But he pressed a finger over my lips. "Sssssh. It's okay," he repeated softly. "It's okay, Nicole."

"Then you know!" I exclaimed. "You know that Lucy and I switched bodies?"

He nodded. "Yes, I know all about it," he said. He wrapped his arm around my shoulders. The arm felt heavy and solid. It felt real.

He isn't a ghost, I thought, staring at him, studying his solemn face. He's really here. He's alive.

"Let's go in the house," he urged, leading me across the tall grass. "Let's go sit down in the house. I'm going to help you, Nicole. That's why I followed you here."

"B-but Lucy—" I stammered.

In my shock at seeing Kent, I had forgotten about her.

I spun away from the barn. I saw her head poke up from inside the well. I saw two pale hands grasping the jagged gray stones at the top.

"Help me!" Lucy called. "Nicole—hurry! I'm slipping. I'm going to fall!"

"Lucy—!" I called to her and started to run.

But Kent grabbed me around the waist and held me back.

"Hurry!" Lucy called. "Hurry, Nicole! I—I can't hold on any longer! I can't!"

Her head disappeared behind the wall of the well. I saw one pale hand slip off.

I had to get to her. I had to save her.

But Kent tightened his grip around my waist.

"Kent—what's *wrong* with you?" I shrieked. "Let me go! Let me go!"

"Let her drown," he murmured in my ear.

chapter

24

"Are you *crazy?*" I cried.

I twisted my body, ducked low, tried to break away.

"Nicole—hurry!" Lucy called, her shrill, frightened voice echoing inside the old well. "Please—hurry! I can't hold on! I can't!"

"Let her drown," Kent repeated coldly, casually, with no emotion at all.

"But she's my friend!" I screamed. "And she's in my body! She's going to drown in my body!"

With a desperate tug I loosened Kent's grip. Then I shot both elbows back hard.

I heard him groan in surprise as my elbows jammed into his stomach.

He let out a weak cry of pain, and his hands dropped away.

I stumbled forward. Fell to my knees. Leaped up.

"Lucy—I'm coming! Hold on! Please—hold on!" I called.

I ran across the grass, my arms outstretched as if reaching for her.

"Hold on! Hold on!" I cried.

My heart thudding, I reached the well.

Grabbed her hand.

Yes. Grabbed it. Got it.

And felt it slip from my grasp. The long red fingernails scratched my palm as the hand slid away.

The hand disappeared from view. I gripped warm air. Nothing but air.

I heard Lucy's terrified scream, all the way down. All the way, all the way. Her echoing scream.

And then a heavy splash.

chapter

25

"*L*ucy! Lucy!"

I didn't even know I was shrieking her name.

I leaned over the side, peered down, down, down, into the darkness.

"Lucy! Lucy!"

The well was so dark, so deep.

I couldn't see her. But I could hear her frantic splashes, hear her short, gasping cries of terror.

I could picture her arms and legs, thrashing wildly, slapping at the water. I could picture her face twisted in horror, arched back out of the water. Sucking in breath after breath.

The water must be so cold, so dirty.

I could picture her hands reaching up, desperately

grabbing at the wet stones of the wall. Slipping off. Slipping off again.

Grabbing and slipping. Grabbing and slipping.

"Lucy! Lucy!"

I could hear the wild thrashing, the echoing splashes. Her desperate, hopeless attempts to stay afloat.

"Help me! Nicole!"

Her voice floated up, ringing as if in a vast cavern. She sounded so far away. Miles and miles away.

She called up only once.

"Lucy—I'm here! Lucy—keep swimming! Lucy—don't give up!" Leaning over the side, staring into the deep darkness, I shouted down to her.

But she didn't call up again.

And the splashing sounds stopped a few seconds later.

And I stared down, feeling the coldness of the stones on my waist, leaned farther down, listening, listening.

Listening to the deep silence.

Listening to her drown.

Drown in my body.

My best friend. Drowned at the bottom of the old well in my body.

I let out a sob as strong hands grabbed my shoulders. Kent pulled me up, away from the well. "Kent—she—she—" I stammered.

He held me gently. Pulled me close. "I know," he whispered. "Nicole, I know."

"I couldn't help her," I choked out, my entire body starting to shake. "I couldn't save her, Kent. I couldn't do anything for her. Nothing at all."

"I know," he repeated tenderly. "I know."

He held me tightly and guided me toward the house.

We were halfway across the yard when Lucy stepped out from behind a tall evergreen shrub.

Her hair fell, wet and tangled with mud and leaves, to her shoulders. Her clothes were soaked, her white tennis shorts stained with mud.

My mouth dropped open. I tried to call her name, but no sound came out.

I felt my knees buckle, my legs go weak, felt myself start to slip to the ground. But Kent held me up, held on to me tightly, as if holding himself up, too.

Walking slowly and deliberately, she stepped in front of us. She pushed the wet, matted hair off her face with both hands.

She had the strangest smile on her pale lips. A pleased smile. A triumphant smile.

"Lucy—!" I finally managed to choke out. "Lucy— how did you get out?"

I wanted to run to her, to throw my arms around her, to hug her and cry for joy.

But her cold smile held me back.

"You—you're out! You're here!" I cried.

Her emerald eyes locked on mine. She didn't utter a sound.

My body is okay, I found myself thinking.

A shameful thought, I know. I should have been

thinking only of my friend. But staring at her—at her in my body—I couldn't help myself.

I couldn't help it. I found myself thinking: *There's still a chance Lucy and I can switch back. Still a chance I can get my own body back from her.*

She moved quickly.

I felt Kent's hand slide off my shoulder as Lucy dived forward.

He uttered a short cry of surprise as Lucy grabbed his head in both hands.

"Let's switch, Kent," Lucy said, her voice watery and strained. "Let's switch—okay?"

Kent tried to pull back.

But Lucy proved too strong for him.

Gripping both sides of his head, she gave it a hard twist—and wrenched the head off his shoulders with one strong tug.

chapter

26

*T*he head made a tearing sound as Lucy ripped it off. Like the scrape of Velcro.

Lucy's eyes lit up and her grin spread across her face as she held Kent's head up high.

I uttered a long howl of terror, of disbelief.

I shut my eyes.

I couldn't bear to see his lifeless head, frozen forever in an expression of shock and horror. I couldn't bear to see Lucy's gleeful grin.

"Let's switch!" Lucy's shrill scream rose into the night air like a wailing siren. "Let's switch! Come on—let's switch!"

I kept my eyes closed. I never wanted to open them again.

"Let's switch!" Lucy shrieked. "Come on, Nicole! You switch heads with Kent—and then I'll switch with you!"

Her high laugh made my entire body shudder.

A few seconds later I heard a car door slam.

I opened my eyes in time to see two men climb out of a black car and come running across the grass. Two gray-suited men.

The Shadyside police officers.

They came charging up beside me. Each of them took one of my arms. Their grip was gentle but firm.

My heart pounded in a wild, unnatural rhythm. My breath caught in my throat. I couldn't speak, couldn't shout out my fear, my terror.

I searched for Lucy and Kent. But they had vanished.

Hearing another car rumble up Grandma Carla's driveway, I turned. The car was filled with people.

All four doors opened at once. I saw my parents climb out and gaze my way. Then I recognized Lucy's parents.

Not dead? The Kramers—not dead?

And then Kent climbed out of the backseat.

They surrounded me quickly, all talking at once.

The two gray-suited men stepped back as my mom threw her arms around me, hugged me, hugged me so tight, weeping, her shoulders trembling. I could feel Mom's hot tears on my face.

"Nicole, Nicole," she whispered my name, pressing her cheek against mine.

When she backed away, Dad hugged me, too.

The two gray-suited men stood tensely at my sides.

Blinking away my own tears, struggling to lift the confusion from my mind, I stared at the Kramers and at Kent.

Not dead.

Not murdered.

All of them alive.

And then I saw Grandma Carla in the middle of the group.

"We're so sorry," Mom was telling her. "We're so sorry Nicole came up here and troubled you. We thought Nicole was okay. We really thought she was over it."

Over it?

What was Mom talking about?

"Nicole has been okay for nearly a year," Mom told Grandma Carla. "No wild nightmares. No hallucinations. No identity problems."

I shook my head, trying to clear it. I desperately wanted to understand Mom, but I couldn't.

I turned and saw Dad talking to Kent. "Kent, that was so good of you to tell us Nicole had slipped again," Dad was saying. "And so decent of you to follow her here. We've had these two doctors from the hospital on her trail." Dad pointed to the gray-suited men. "But we never would have found Nicole without you."

Hospital workers?

They weren't police officers?

Kent muttered something, his eyes on the ground. I couldn't hear what he said.

They were all talking at once. It was so hard to understand.

I turned to see Grandma Carla shake her head fretfully. "Poor Lucy has been dead for three years," she said sadly. "That horrible, horrible car accident . . ." Her voice trailed off. She let out a long sigh.

"Nicole started having the hallucinations right after Lucy died," Mom explained to her. "She started seeing horrible deaths. They were all in her mind. But they were so real to her."

Grandma Carla *tsk-tsked*, shaking her head sadly.

My mom continued: "After Lucy died, Nicole started talking to her, imagining that Lucy was still with her. And sometimes . . . sometimes . . ."

Mom's voice caught in her throat. She swallowed hard. "Sometimes Nicole even imagines that she *is* Lucy," she told Grandma Carla.

"She just can't accept the fact that Lucy has been dead for three years," Dad added sadly.

"You'll get her the help she needs," Grandma Carla replied softly. "She'll be okay. I'm sure."

They continued talking. Their voices blended into each other. Became just sound to me.

I didn't really care what they were saying. I felt happy now.

I felt happy to see them. Happy and relieved that I didn't have to run anymore. Happy that everyone was alive and okay.

So happy that I didn't even put up a fight as the two gray-suited men led me to their car.

chapter

27

*T*hat happened nearly six months ago. Now I'm doing really well.

I'm feeling so much better. My nightmares have stopped. I haven't had one in weeks and weeks. I sleep so peacefully now. Like a baby.

I haven't seen any more horrible murders. I realize now that they were all in my mind, all just frightening hallucinations.

They seemed so real. I believed them to be true.

But I know better now.

The ugly hallucinations are behind me. And I intend to keep them behind me.

I have such a positive attitude. I feel so good about myself lately.

I guess the main reason I feel so wonderful is that Lucy comes to visit me every day.

Such a good friend. She hasn't missed a single day.

It has meant so much to me. Seeing Lucy at my bedside every day has really helped to speed my recovery.

I think the doctors are going to let me out soon.

Won't that be great, Lucy?

Maybe they'll let me go back to school in time for graduation. And you and I will graduate together.

That will be just perfect—won't it, Lucy?

That will be just perfect.

Don't you agree?

About the Author

R.L. Stine invented the teen horror genre with Fear Street, the bestselling teen horror series of all time. He also changed the face of children's publishing with the mega-successful Goosebumps series, which *Guinness World Records* cites as the Best-Selling Children's Book Series ever, and went on to become a worldwide multimedia phenomenon. The first two books in his new series Mostly Ghostly, *Who Let the Ghosts Out?* and *Have You Met My Ghoulfriend?*, are *New York Times* bestsellers. He's thrilled to be writing for teens again in the brand-new Fear Street Nights books.

R.L. Stine has received numerous awards of recognition, including several Nickelodeon Kids' Choice Awards and Disney Adventures Kids' Choice Awards, and he has been selected by kids as one of their favorite authors in the National Education Association Read Across America. He lives in New York City with his wife, Jane, and their dog, Nadine.

DEAR READERS,

WELCOME TO FEAR STREET—WHERE YOUR WORST NIGHTMARES LIVE! IT'S A TERRIFYING PLACE FOR SHADYSIDE HIGH STUDENTS—AND FOR YOU!

DID YOU KNOW THAT THE SUN NEVER SHINES ON THE OLD MANSIONS OF FEAR STREET? NO BIRDS CHIRP IN THE FEAR STREET WOODS. AND AT NIGHT, EERIE MOANS AND HOWLS RING THROUGH THE TANGLED TREES.

I'VE WRITTEN NEARLY A HUNDRED FEAR STREET NOVELS, AND I AM THRILLED THAT MILLIONS OF READERS HAVE ENJOYED ALL THE FRIGHTS AND CHILLS IN THE BOOKS. WHEREVER I GO, KIDS ASK ME WHEN I'M GOING TO WRITE A NEW FEAR STREET TRILOGY.

WELL, NOW I HAVE SOME EXCITING NEWS. I HAVE WRITTEN A BRAND-NEW FEAR STREET TRILOGY. THE THREE NEW BOOKS ARE CALLED FEAR STREET NIGHTS. THE SAGA OF SIMON AND ANGELICA FEAR AND THE UNSPEAKABLE EVIL THEY CAST OVER THE TEENAGERS OF SHADYSIDE WILL CONTINUE IN THESE NEW BOOKS. YES, SIMON AND ANGELICA FEAR ARE BACK TO BRING TERROR TO THE TEENS OF SHADYSIDE.

FEAR STREET NIGHTS IS AVAILABLE NOW. . . . DON'T MISS IT. I'M VERY EXCITED TO RETURN TO FEAR STREET—AND I HOPE YOU WILL BE THERE WITH ME FOR ALL THE GOOD, SCARY FUN!

RL Stine

feel the fear.

FEAR STREET® NIGHTS

A brand-new Fear Street trilogy by the master of horror

R.L. STINE

In Stores Now

Simon Pulse
Published by Simon & Schuster
FEAR STREET is a registered trademark of Parachute Press, Inc.

FEAR STREET ®

WHERE YOUR WORST NIGHTMARES LIVE

- ALL-NIGHT PARTY
- THE CONFESSION
- FIRST DATE
- KILLER'S KISS
- THE PERFECT DATE
- THE RICH GIRL
- SECRET ADMIRER
- THE STEPSISTER
- SWITCHED
- THE BEST FRIEND

SWITCHED

THE BEST FRIEND

By bestselling author

R.L. STINE

Simon Pulse
Published by Simon & Schuster
FEAR STREET is a registered trademark of Parachute Press, Inc.